The ELFQUEST GATHERUM

Volume Two

Edited by
Richard Pini

ANOTHER ONE, NONNA! NEXT THEY'LL BE COMING OUT OF THE CAVE WALLS!

FATHER
TREE
PRESS
Poughkeepsie,
New York

The Elfquest Gatherum, Volume Two

ISBN 0-936861-03-7
Published by Father Tree Press, a division of Warp Graphics, Inc.
Design & Production: Richard Pini
Copyright © 1988 Warp Graphics, Inc.

First printing: April 1988
10 9 8 7 6 5 4 3 2 1

Printed in U.S.A.

Contents

Cover: Hot fun in the summertime. Painting by Wendy Pini.

Page 4: Introduction
A short tour through the ten year history of Elfquest.

Page 6: The Other Mountain
by Richard Meyers
A second introduction, in the form of a reminiscence.

Page 10: A Day In The Lives
Elves couldn't really exist in modern day Poughkeepsie, could they?

Page 20: Research into Elfquest
by Ree Moorhead Pruehs
A brief sourcebook for emulating the lifestyles of the short and feral.

Page 32: Getting Bent
by Wendy Pini
A primer on elf-think for those who are not.

Page 38: Portfolio
Six scenes from the World of Two Moons, elegantly rendered.

Page 45: Further Conversations with WaRP
Two interviews with Wendy and Richard Pini, on a variety of topics.

Page 76: Games People Play
Artwork from the Elfquest role-playing game and supplements.

Page 82: Recognition
by Richard Pini
A reptilian explanation for this undeniable attraction.

Page 88: From Elfland to Tinseltown (part 2)
The further adventures of the Wolfriders in their quest to lead a more animated life.

Page 98: Potpourri
Various and sundry bits from the pencil/pen/brush of Wendy Pini

Page 108: The Woman Wolfriders
by Deborah Dunn
Don't dare call them the weaker sex or try to keep them in the kitchen!

Page 120: The Elfquest Glossary (part 2)
From Adar to Zwoot, a collection of terms from the world of the elves.

Page 144: Outroduction
Parting words and a look forward to the next ten years.

Back cover: Cutter and Nightrunner. Pastel by Wendy Pini.

Introduction:
a kind of primer

For the new reader, and perhaps even for the old, the very first information in this book should be a simple and concise history of the various incarnations of *Elfquest*. For the title and its connected stories have been through sufficient permutations that, without a scorecard, the unwary may get confused. (And, after ten years, even the editor sometimes feels a bit unwary!)

The chronology is as follows:

• 1978-1984 — Warp Graphics publishes the independent comic book *Elfquest* — the story of a tribe of elves called the Wolfriders — as a 20-issue, magazine sized (which is to say, about 8 1/2 by 11 inches) black and white series. *Elfquest* is distributed only through comics specialty shops. These issues are now long out of print and hard to find.

• 1981-1984 — The Donning Company publishes *Elfquest* Books One through Four which are compiled and colorized versions of the Warp Graphics comics.

• 1981 — Fantagraphics Books publishes the *Elfquest Gatherum*, an encyclopedia *cum* family album containing articles and artwork that relate to Elfquest.

•1982 — Berkley publishes *Journey to Sorrow's End*, which is a novelization of the first part of the Elfquest saga.

•1985-1988 — Marvel Comics publishes *Elfquest* in a 32-issue series of comic book sized color issues reprinting all of the original Warp Graphics material with the addition of new artwork done specially for this series. These comics are available on newsstands as well as in comics shops.

•1986 — Tor Books publishes *Blood of Ten Chiefs*, the first volume in a series of shared-universe anthologies, featuring well-known science fiction and fantasy authors, and based on the early world of Elfquest. In 1988, the second volume *Wolfsong* is released.

•1986 — Warp Graphics produces a new Elfquest comics story entitled *Siege at Blue Mountain*, which continues the adventures of the Wolfriders. *Siege* is a comic sized, black and white series of eight issues.

•1988 — Elfquest is ten years old! Father Tree Press (a "branch" of Warp Graphics) publishes the *Elfquest Gatherum* Volume Two.

•1988-1989 — To celebrate Elfquest's 10th anniversary, Father Tree Press publishes newly recolored and revised editions of the old color volumes, adding new artwork that has not previously appeared in the Donning editions. Father Tree also expands the series from four to six volumes to include the material contained in *Siege at Blue Mountain*. The six Graphic Novel volume titles are: *Fire and Flight*, *The Forbidden Grove*, *Captives of Blue Mountain*, *Quest's End*, *Siege at Blue Mountain*, and *The Secret of Two-Edge*.

Ten years...

So why a second volume of the Gatherum? Ah, an easy question for a change. Back in 1981, when Volume One (of course, we didn't *know* it was just "Volume One" at that time) was first published, the original Warp Graphics *Elfquest* story was about half completed. Yes, we knew there was more story to come, but it seemed to us that the content of the *Gatherum* was sufficiently general and far-reaching that it would serve for the entire series.

Well, we'd been wrong before, too.

As it turned out, the story, the world, the characters grew in complexity and fascination all beyond our original expectations. Plot threads twisted and turned in new directions. Personalities that started out simple "got bent" and became convoluted. More and more an element of autobiography entered the picture, adding another dimension onto the structure of the tale. Elfquest evolved into a multi-layered experience that could be read as a simple fairy tale, an adventure story, or a psychological parable. The elves turned out to be a lot more versatile than we thought!

And there were unexpected events happening outside the boundaries of the printed page as well. Elfquest was beginning to enjoy a measure of success previously unknown in the independent comics field. A major publishing house in New York wanted a novelization of the story. An animation studio in Canada wanted to talk about producing an animated film. A game company wanted to develop a role-playing game. Another independent publisher wanted to publish a portfolio of artwork based on the series...

Things were changing, and changing at a rapid pace, for Wendy and Richard Pini of Poughkeepsie, New York. And it's clear now, seven years after the publication of the first *Gatherum*, that one just isn't going to be enough. There have been more than enough experiences and changes and ups and downs and new things to see to fill a second volume. And *that* (in abbreviated form, for the real meat is just past these opening pages) is why there's a Volume Two.

Ten years...

Having just reread the introduction that I wrote for Volume One, I find myself face to face with the truth of the old adage, the more things change, the more they stay the same. Certainly the face of comics in America has undergone a marked change since 1978 — or 1981. But I wonder how much the *substance* has grown, if at all. Then, taking it down to a more personal level, I read my seven-year-old words about feeling burnt out — *there's* something with which I know Wendy and I are both still familiar! Our style of working together has become quite different, as has the way in which each issue of the comic book is produced — but the old love and excitement is still there. It strikes us a bit differently, but it's the same feeling.

Ten years is a long time, and it isn't. There are people who have worked on projects for that long, and longer — but then, there aren't many of them in the field of comics. Certainly not in the arena of the independent comics. In fact, I like to think of things in terms of the fact that *Elfquest* is ten years old this year. So are the "indies." This, I do not see as coincidence.

Happy 10th, everyone.

— Richard Pini

The Other Mountain

an introduction of sorts
in a personal vein
by Richard Meyers

Elves came into my life early. I was idly wondering, as I was wont to do, what life was like before glasses. Having almost always worn thick spectacles, I couldn't help but wonder what it would have been like had I been born into a time without them. Did you ever notice that characters who *do* live in the era before glasses never need them? Which came first? Glasses or astigmatism?

It's fodder for an observational comedian like Jerry Sienfeld or Paul Reiser. How come nobody from the 1600s back was ever near- or farsighted? That was the question I asked myself, and from that came my first grand script idea. I wedded that casual consideration to my theory that all mythical creations have some basis in fact to come up with a fantasy epic: the tale of a nearsighted, disgraced court jester discovering the remnants of an elfin civilization.

It would be a tragic adventure, I decided, as the court jester fell in love with the female offspring of the only interspecies marriage of elf and human — and this would signal the end of elfin civilization. An angry, envious king would declare war on the elves since they were effortlessly happy and he was consumed with neuroses. The court jester would defeat the king with magic, but the elves' population would be so depleted that they could not survive to modern times.

Although the jester would be heartbroken, his last elf friends would assure him it was just as well — elves could never coexist with humanity. Elves knew how to celebrate life. Humans seemed to need to be miserable. The jester would be left as the elves had found him — alone, in the snow. Still, the audience's tears should've been tempered with joy. The jester had found love, had defeated evil, and had learned something about how to live.

I never actually wrote it, of course. I knew enough about the movie business to know that the script would be hopelessly expensive and impossible to cast. Hollywood elves never looked any good. Besides, my heart wasn't in it. Although I could empathize with nearsightedness, I never liked elves all that much. I had more in common with the evil king: elves were too cute...too uncomplicated...too "perfect".

Sometimes I would tell the story of the nearsighted court jester around a fire at Farm Camp Lowy in Windsor, New York, or on a camping trip,

6

but I dropped it as a viable money-making project. Instead, I started to write articles for *Cinefantastique* and *Starlog*, book proposals for Pinnacle and Charter Publications, and comic book plots for Seaboard/Atlas.

The latter company hired me as Assistant Editor, where I stayed for a year before moving over to *Starlog* as Associate Editor. Between the two I gathered college credits in Bridgeport, Connecticut and Boston. And somewhere in there I got a package in the mail from Richard Pini.

I had been friends with Richard's brother, Carl, through high school, and we would jump the stone fence behind the Pinis' home to enact fantasy adventures on the adjoining golf course. It wasn't until college that Carl suggested I visit Richard, who was then working at the Boston Museum of Science's Planetarium. The Planetarium? I liked the man already. Here he was, doing what I wanted to do, working with his head in the stars!

We got along fine, and while we didn't do any heavy hanging out together, we kept in touch. So I wasn't exactly stunned when I got the package containing the first two issues of *Fantasy Quarterly* and *Elfquest* and a letter. As I recall, the personal missive said that Richard and Wendy wanted to get all sorts of feedback from their friends and fellow professionals. To paraphrase: what did I think?

Well, sir. If memory serves, I had just finished a rough half-year snarling at Atlas Comics where Jeff Rovin was desperately trying to save the dozen comic books he had fathered and nurtured. I had spent this half year watching wonderful work by Michael Kaluta, Howard Chaykin, Walt Simonson, Jeff Jones, Larry Hama, Neal Adams, Pat Broderick and many, many others, being turned into junk for the most petty, ludicrous, and arbitrary reasons by the most short-sighted publishers I had ever worked for.

I had been guided to the top of the mountain, then thrown off the cliff. I was going to be a part of the greatest thing that ever happened to comics since Stan Lee. I was going to be one of the innovators in a new line of mature comic books which would set new standards for writing and art. I was going to be one of the ones to bring new depth and emotion to the medium. I was going to be an editor who unlocked the secrets of the form. Me, me, me!

Instead, I toiled over an increasingly degenerating batch of titles which worsened in quality the more the noncreative members of the staff interfered. I was sickened, I was disgusted, I was burned out. At one point I actually walked into the men's room with a pair of scissors and cut off most of my hair. Jeff was not able to sublimate his emotions as well. He nearly had a physical breakdown instead. We were going to do something great, and instead were attached to something miserable.

So, maybe my excuse is that the last thing I wanted to see at that moment was another comic book. Especially one with such beautiful elves. I remember thinking: *look at those chests.* In the words of the comedian, so round, so firm, so fully packed! And that was just the males.

I vaguely remember my answering letter to the Pinis. Too predictable, I said. Too facile. Too pretty. Too pat. As I think about it now, what I was actually saying was that they acted too much like elves! What I wanted to do was make "my" elves more human, more untraditionally flawed. But these weren't my elves, of course, and I should have been stunned and gratified that these two people actually went out and achieved something Atlas couldn't with all its millions. I should have been supportive whatever my personal misgivings were.

But as I said, elves weren't my cup of tea. And after Atlas, neither were comics.

I went away for almost ten years. I watched as Atlas died, its only legacy being to raise artists' and writers' pay rates. After that I couldn't bear to look at a comic book. The grand experiment had failed, killed by the "Golden Rule" (whoever has the former makes the latter). The ultimate tragedy was that Atlas was not killed by competition, but by its own in-house strangulation. Marvel and DC were left to monopolize the business and have the artists dance to their tune.

I wrote books. Nonfiction hardcovers as well as fiction paperbacks. I wrote under every name but my own. I merely touched upon comics again in 1979 when I was the only non-Marvel employee to write a Marvel novel for Pocket Books (*The Incredible Hulk: Cry of the Beast*). I moved forward, without looking back, to enter the science-fiction field with three nonfiction books and two novels. I spoke at conventions. I ghost-wrote a slasher movie. I worked on television.

Finally I stumbled back into comics. The last late, lamented Manhattan Empiricon convention had but a single comics panel, which needed a moderator. Since most of the panelists were old pals from the Atlas days, I willingly volunteered. Howard Chaykin was in the audience and Walt Simonson suggested I get him up there to talk about his comic which was about to premiere: *American Flagg!* Walt couldn't say enough about it and the entire experience reminded me of how much fun comics could be.

It also reminded me of the goals I was hoping to accomplish through Atlas. So I took a look at issue one of *American Flagg!* and was hopelessly hooked again. I ignored my existential pain and dove back into the industry — only this time as an observer and an audience, which is really the best job of all.

I continued writing books, but read comics voraciously. I got a professional discount at Forbidden Planet, the largest comic book store in the English-speaking world. I became a creative consultant to the Dream Factory, the largest comic book store in Connecticut. I bought comics in Paris, Hong Kong and Tokyo.

I had come back at the right time. The industry was about to burst wide open. There was about to be an orgy of creativity which would unleash comics' Platinum Age. And once I examined the causes and effects, there was one undeniable fact: if *Elfquest* wasn't the explosive trigger, then it was, at least, the fuse.

Everywhere I went, I saw the effects. *Elfquest* comics, *Elfquest* magazines, and *Elfquest* books. Plans for an *Elfquest* movie, *Elfquest* toys, an *Elfquest* television show. But that really wasn't the important thing — not to me, at any rate. The important thing was the effect *Elfquest* had on the comic industry. It wasn't as if Richard and Wendy set out to prove anything to the big boys, to humiliate or embarrass them. The one thing I saw in *Elfquest* was (dare I say it?) love.

Again and again, in my books and magazine columns, I maintain that it takes only two things to make character drama work. Those things aren't good looks or relevance. They aren't marketing and pandering to the lowest common denominator. They are *passion* and *compassion*. Richard and Wendy's passion was obvious in every word and picture. Their characters' compassion was obvious in every panel. This was lush, romantic, engrossing stuff which I was not prepared for or interested in.

But I was an exception. *Elfquest* found its audience in those who passionately and compassionately cared about elves. Sure, I clapped to keep Tinker Bell alive, but I did so reluctantly. Hell, I wasn't going to have the blood of no elf on my conscience! But still, I was more interested in the nearsighted court jester than the race of mythical creatures he was partly responsible for destroying.

Beyond story considerations, however, I credit *Elfquest* for opening up the comics industry because Wendy and Richard proved that an independent comic could not just make thousands of people care, it could make money. Lots of money. So much money that the comics corporations not only sat up, not only paid attention, but paid cash! The companies which had scoffed at the Pinis' chances before now wanted a piece of the *Elfquest* pie.

The Pinis had also helped the industry blossom because they had inspired dozens of others to go the independent route, to give life to their own passions, unhindered by the "Dark Side's Golden Rule."

The trick is to care. The trick is to be true to yourself. The trick is to do something for some reason other than just money. The trick is to work hard and finish it. The trick is not to listen to anyone who says it's too predictable and too facile. If you can do that, you can move mountains.

Elfquest has changed the comic world. Without it, there might have been no *American Flagg!*, no *Love and Rockets*, no *Concrete*, no *Elektra*, maybe not even a *Dark Knight* or *Watchmen*. Because the Pinis proved there was a market for something other than just full figures in action. There was a market for words, for deep emotions, for something other than "comic book" art.

It's cold up here on my mountain top. Cold and lonely. I sit here and type without the comfort of elves. They died out of my world many years ago. I must lean down close to the page to see it clearly. I am nearsighted and have no glasses.

In the distance I hear laughter and singing. It's coming from that other mountain, the blue one. I hear the sounds of joy and sadness, of peace and war. I hear life from that mountain.

There is no life here. Only work. But maybe, with time, the elves that live on that other mountain can teach me something. Maybe they can help me see what many others have seen clearly. Work isn't work if you love it.

Richard Meyers wrote the *Year of the Ninja Master* novels under the name Wade Barker for Warner Books, as well as the best-selling nonfiction work *Martial Arts Movies from Bruce Lee to the Ninjas* for Citadel Press in 1984. He was "Special Media Consultant" for the new *Twilight Zone* series on CBS in 1985. He traveled to the Orient to make the videos *This is Kung Fu* and *Ninja Mania* in 1986. He started writing the *War of the Ninja Master* novels in 1987. The first of these, *The Kohga Ritual*, was published in January of 1988. The second, *The Shibo Discipline*, appeared in May, with more to follow. He reviews television for *The Armchair Detective* magazine and comics for *Mystery Scene*.

A Day in the Lives

It has been said that one should take one's work more seriously than one takes oneself. It has also been said that one should not take anything *too* seriously. There were times, during the telling of the original *Elfquest* series, that the work and the world seemed to get very serious indeed. Since Wendy and Richard had long maintained that it was so easy to tell the elves' story because the little folk actually lived with them, perhaps it was only natural that cartoons chronicling the "real life" adventures of Cutter and crew started appearing in the back pages of the comics. The "Day in the Lives" vignettes certainly helped to keep things in a kind of perspective, and provided a gently humorous safety valve for when the pressure got high. It's all in good fun. Except...the neighbors can be heard, now and then, muttering, "It's only a comic book; it's only a comic book..."

"I'D LIKE TWO HUNDRED POUNDS OF WOLF CHOW, AND ALL THE SHORT LEASHES YOU'VE GOT!"

Research into Elfquest
or: Living like the Wolfriders
(as closely as possible)

by Ree Moorhead Pruehs

Of course you know that no one is really thrusting swords through the magician's lovely assistant who is locked in a trunk onstage, no matter how convincing her screams or the blood gleaming upon the blades. In spite of that, though, don't you feel a thrill of nervous anticipation until she emerges alive and whole? And wouldn't you feel cheated — even angry at the magician's incompetence — if the trunk were to fly open halfway through the trick, allowing you to see that it isn't real, after all? Would you really want to watch the rest of his act?

If you are a creator, whether writer, artist, or gamesmaster, you have the same obligation to your audience as the above mentioned magician. Should the reader/viewer/participant catch an error in your creation, you run the risk of that trunk flying open — and along with it, a lost audience. *But it's fantasy*, you say? So it is. But that simply means that by the laws of this world we live upon the tale you're telling can't or likely won't happen. It does not mean you can allow your world to be internally illogical or inconsistent.

The first rule of writing is, traditionally, *Write What You Know*. But this isn't totally inflexible. You don't really have to be on personal speaking terms with a wolf, know a poultice from an infusion, or be able to knapp a razor-sharp knife from a couple of rocks to write about the subjects. Even if your honest-to-Gotara idea of "roughing it" is staying in an off-brand motel instead of the Hilton, there is hope for you. Behold the dread goddess who shall breathe life into your creations, and do not fear her: her name is *Research*.

"*But research is dull!*" you cry. Given the proper inspiration — your desire to write — and the proper material, it doesn't have to be. Let's head for the bookshelves, shall we? (If your shelves don't groan as heavily as ours, your local library, bolstered by interlibrary loans, can often produce an amazing amount of material on topics you'd never dreamed existed...outside the pages of *Elfquest*, that is.)

First of all, a caution: never lose track of the idea that if you're going to work with the World of Two Moons (hereafter **WoTM**), you are working within the confines of someone else's dream. "Improving" upon the original does not make for good pastiche; it isn't your world to improve upon. So go back to the source: the original *Elfquest* and its sequel, the novelization *Journey to Sorrow's End*, and published interviews with Wendy and Richard Pini. Of lesser importance and/or reliability (albeit still valuable for inspiration and background) are the *Elfquest* role-playing games and the *Blood of Ten Chiefs* anthologies.

Find yourself a good set of writer's tools — no, I don't mean the latest, gizmo-laden word processor on the market. Get a good dictionary and thesaurus. There are too many types of each to name. Browse in a bookstore until you find one or more of each that suit you.

Now, to **WoTM** specifics.

A quick, easy way to get another perspective on the right "word feel" is the excellent *Earth's Children* series by Jean M. Auel (published by Berkley Books). It's set in the right time and technology period, it's entertaining, it's accurate (*well, reasonably accurate; some anthropologists roll their eyes up at the series - Ed.*) — Auel really makes the era, especially the crafts and skills practiced by her primitive humans, come alive. A warning — these are good thick books; don't get started on one if you have something else to do.

Do you want to learn the skills, crafts, and many of the philosophies of the **WoTM** elves for yourself? It isn't cheap — four to five hundred dollars a class, as of mid-1987 — but the classes exist. Tom Brown, Jr. began his "apprenticeship" in forest lore at the age of eight, guided by the Apache elder Stalking Wolf. After being featured in *People* magazine, he disappeared into the wilderness and spent a year there with only a knife for equipment. Today he runs the **Tracking, Nature and Wilderness Survival School.** (Send a SASE — self-addressed stamped envelope — for information to The Tracker, PO Box 318, Milford NJ 08848.)

Not that ambitious? Refer to Brown's excellent series of trade-edition paperback "Field Guides"; I find the complete collection the single most important set of references for *Elfquest* writing, art or gaming. In fact, if I were to name the single most helpful reference book for use in writing *Elfquest* stories, it would probably be *Tom Brown's Field Guide to Wilderness Survival*, with *Tom Brown's Guide to Living With the Earth* a very close runner-up (the first covers more subjects, the second explores its topics in more loving detail and goes further into philosophy). Covered topics in *Wilderness Survival*, by chapter, are: Attitude, Shelter, Water, Fire, Plants (listing one hundred edible plants and a chart of general plant habitats), Animals (from hunting ethics to skinning, cleaning and utilizing the entire animal carcass), Cooking and Preserving, Tools and Crafts, Cautions and Suggestions (for the modern reader). These books do not exceed the given technology of the WoTM in any way (the only tool it is supposed you start with is a knife), and cover all aspects of "living with the earth". The books are simple to read and understand, and are so beautifully told you're likely to forget you're doing research. They are also crammed with useful information, philosophy, and clear line drawings of the crafts, tracks, skills or plants being spoken of. (The other books in the series deal with tracking, plant life, and nature observation; see the list in the bibliography.)

In addition, Brown's autobiographical novels *The Search* and *The Tracker* furnish far more interesting scenario ideas than the standard *Elfquest* fan-tale of elves jumped by packs of random Gotara-worshipping humans.

Not the pause that refreshes? Oh, well...

There are other survival books readily available. Most of the following are easily located — generally you can find one or more in any given B. Dalton's or Waldenbooks store. All are paperbacks, some are mass-market editions: the *U.S. Armed Forces Survival Manual*, Bradford Angier's *Survival With Style*, Richard Graves's *Bushcraft: A Serious Guide to Survival and Camping*, and Larry Dean Olsen's *Outdoor Survival Skills*. None of these are as lovingly detailed or as entertaining to read as the Brown books, but all are handy, reasonably inexpensive, one-book source guides. A caveat: use all of the above books with discretion as they utilize technology not yet developed on the WoTM; the "water stills" made with plastic sheeting are reasonably apparent as such, but other devices spoken of are equally unusable but not as obvious. (A digression/commentary on *Elfquest Book 1*, taken from *Outdoor Survival Skills* — "A cactus can be cut and peeled and the moisture sucked out, but this is not the same as drinking running water — it is more like drinking Elmer's Glue." Poor Wolfriders!)

Also available, if not completely useful, are the trilogy of books published by *Muzzleloader* magazine: *The Book*

22

of Buckskinning Volumes I, II and III. Forget the gunpowder; it doesn't work on the **WoTM** anyway, by decree of the High Ones. Concentrate on the articles on brain-tanning buckskin, quillworking, horseback travel and tomahawk/knife throwing. I've also found many interesting things in John Seymour's *The Guide to Self Sufficiency.* Many *Elfquest* writers seem to find the Foxfire series of books helpful; virtually every bookstore carries one or more of the volumes. Again, though, these books utilize technology "outside the limits" and none of these volumes is comprehensive in and of itself.

As long as weapons have crept in here, let's talk about them. Weapons combat skill and hunting skill are different disciplines involving different motivations; an elf skilled in one may not be much good for the other! So far as weapons combat skill is concerned, many fantasy writers and artists — professional as well as fan — seem influenced by the Indiana Jones School of Swordplay (e.g., what they see on TV and in the movies) when creating scenes involving personal combat. Many sword-and-sorcery flicks are actually pretty laughable, all glitz, unusable weaponry and little if any actual technique. (That the "thrust to the heart works every time = instant kill" is one of the great fictional myths. It's actually pretty hard to hit the heart with a blade weapon, as a little thought and anatomy study will confirm. The breastbone and ribs tend to get in the way. The throat or the wrists are far more vulnerable targets on an unarmed person.)

Granted, I have certain advantages for weapons reference that many folks don't; my husband studies and teaches different forms of weapons combat, is an armorer and knifemaker by hobby, loves his crafts, and can happily give a twenty minute lecture/demonstration on such topics as "The Proper Use of the Spear in Troll/Elf Combat". You can get to know similarly talented people by contacting your local branch of the **Society for Creative Anachronism**, an international organization that specializes in medieval research and re-creation. The SCA has chapters in or near most good-sized cities and/or universities.

Roland Green (author, reviewer, and an *Elfquest* fan) once said that a combination of observing SCA fighting, combined with thorough research, is the best way to figure out how weapons combat "really works", and I've always found his advice sound. Re-creation of tournament combat is one of the things for which the SCA is best known, although SCA members also practice many other skills of the medieval/ Renaissance time period - herbalism, dancing, illumination, calligraphy, costuming, brewing and feasting, just to name a few. To locate the group nearest you write: Registrar, Society for Creative Anachronism, Inc., Office of the Registry, PO Box 360743, Milpitas CA 95035-0743. Enclose a SASE.

If research is all you're after, though, ask the local group if you may attend a fighting practice. Tournaments are fun, but you can't really ask the fighters to "stop and do it again, would you?" Observe, take notes — and pictures, if you've asked permission. Be courteous and offer to bear water to hot, thirsty fighters. Wait until there appears to be a break in the action before asking questions of the person in charge. Most fighting SCA members, when not actually beating on each other, are more than willing to talk about the finer points of their hobby. Want to learn the arts of weapons combat for yourself? Go for it! In most cases, all you'll need to do is ask. The other fighters will be glad to help you get started — and oh yes, in the SCA women fight, too. I should mention, however, that for legal reasons most groups are prohibited from training minors in weapons combat.

Books on related subjects? Dan Inosanto's *The Filipino Martial Arts* and *Absorb What Is Useful* demonstrate many aspects of striking and defense. (Inosanto, a professional stuntman and protege of Bruce Lee, runs a school in California and teaches seminars across the country.)

Ignore the silly title and cover of *Traditional Ninja Weapons: Fighting Techniques of the Shadow Warrior* by Charles Daniel, but don't ignore the book. Inside are clear pictures and accompanying descriptions of several forms of weapons combat, including knife, staff and sword fighting. The SCA publication *The Fighter's Handbook* is also helpful to the novice, though it necessarily overconcentrates on shield work and armor requirements. The researcher can also look for other books about the Filipino martial arts **arnis**, **kali** and **escrima** (stick fighting), as well as volumes that focus on the use of the **Bo** staff (similar to a quarterstaff). Some books on the latter are listed in the bibliography. A good basic book on the use of the bow and arrow is *Archery for Beginners* by John C. Williams, a gold medal Olympast and an Olympic archery coach. (Bow and arrow construction may be found in Brown's *Living with the Earth*, mentioned above.)

The astute will notice that I've recommended no books on unarmed combat. It is my feeling that this type of combat — except for basic arts such as wrestling — is unlikely to develop in most **WoTM** cultures. On Earth, most of today's unarmed combat forms were developed in response to the needs of warrior cultures of a higher social and technological level than that of the average Wolfrider tribe. It would appear, too, that unarmed combat would do elves little good except against their own kind. Humans have a considerable reach and mass advantage over the elves, while trolls appear to have a lesser reach advantage and a greater mass advantage.

Don't go by what you see on TV or in some schlock kung-fu movie, either. Movie combat is carefully choreographed to look good for the camera — it has little to do with "real life" fighting. See the Inosanto book *Absorb What Is Useful*. If you are considering elf *sans* weapons against troll, think about a combat-trained man throwing kicks and blows at a sumo wrestler. The normal man bounces. Real life Bruce Lees are few and far between — and that sort of talent takes years of intensive study and discipline first to acquire and then to maintain. Survival, not warmaking, seems the elves' main goal on the **WoTM**. And unarmed combat is basically useless for hunting.

Unfortunately, the prime result of fighting is that someone usually ends up getting hurt. The result of blows or cuts to a given area of the anatomy may be found in or gathered from such books as Bruce Tegner's *Self-defense Nerve Centers and Pressure Points* or N. Mashiro's excellent *Black Medicine: the Dark Art of Death* series. Warning: the latter is very graphic and decidedly not for the squeamish. Symptoms and treatment of specific injuries, such as fractures or frostbite, can be found in any of a number of excellent medical guides on the mass market.

Do I hear a question about why elves would need to know first aid, since they have psychokinetic healers? I ask in return: What happens when the healer is unavailable, exhausted, distracted or nonexistent?

A good all-around first aid textbook is the American Red Cross's *Standard First Aid and Personal Safety*, readily available in most bookstores or as part of the package acquired by taking a Multimedia First Aid class at your local Red Cross center. A community service note: this course takes eight hours of your life, often less, costs under $20 and could save someone's life. Wolfriders aren't the only ones who need to be prepared for the unexpected. Besides, didn't you need a break from that typewriter anyway?

Other books I continually return to are: The American Medical Association's *Handbook of First Aid and Emergency Care, Emergency Medical Guide* by John Henderson, and *Concise Book of Outdoor First Aid* by Terry Brown and Rob Hunter.

While we're on the subject of medical reference, I shouldn't neglect *The Merck Manual*, one of the best-known and most readily available medical textbooks. Although it falls somewhat short on injury/shock reference, no other book really comes close on just about any other medical topic, particularly diseases. Unfortunately, even in paperback the book is expensive. Try to find a copy in a library or used book store. The manual also makes for dry, technical reading; you may want to have a medical dictionary handy.

Pharmacology on the WoTM is, essentially, herbalism. Billed as "the most complete catalogue of nature's miracle plants ever published", *The Herb Book* by John Lust is a 600+ page paperback jammed with facts and more than 275 line drawings of plants. Most herb descriptions include the common name, medicinal parts, description, properties and uses, and preparation/dosage information. A separate section lists herbs that are used for natural dyes. *Living Medicine: the Healing Properties of Plants* by Mannfried Paahlow is not nearly as comprehensive but does have larger drawings than the Lust book, and pretty color plates.

Other uses of plants are discussed in *Earth Medicine, Earth Food* by Michael A. Weiner, which examines the plant remedies, drugs, and natural foods of the North American Indians. What is particularly fascinating about this book are the extra tidbits and anecdotes that make the herbal research more interesting for modern readers — for example: you may have read that primitive tribes drink willow-bark tea to cure fevers. Did you know that our modern-day aspirin is chemically related to the salicylic acid found in fresh willow bark? A different look at the same topic is provided in Frances Densmore's *How Indians Use Wild Plants for Food, Medicine and Crafts.* Information on dyeing processes may be found in Elijah Bemiss' *The Dyer's Companion.*

The last two books mentioned are produced by **Dover Publications**, which

Don't get caught in this situation! Learn those herbs!

Pharmacology, Bone Woman style.

bears mention in its own right. Dover produces over 200 books per year on a variety of topics, often publishing facsimile editions of books long out-of-print. *The Dyer's Companion*, for example, was originally printed in 1815. Dover reproduces the original text intact, adding an introduction and appendices by the curator of the Smithsonian Institution's Division of Textiles. Nearly all Dover books are inexpensive, high-quality paperbacks. A free catalog may be obtained by writing them directly: Dover Publications, Inc., 31 East 2nd Street, Mineola NY 11501.

Quite often where there are elves, there are wolves. Barry Holstun Lopez's *Of Wolves and Men* has more than once been described as "the bible" of wolf books. I agree — if you only have one book on wolves, this should be it. This beautifully illustrated, comprehensive volume covers not only description, pack social structure, communication and hunting habits of the wolves, but their relationship with man, and man's attitudes towards wolves. It will inspire you. Be warned: it will also anger and sadden you. Also recommended: *The Wolf*, by Michael Fox, a narrative story about a pack and pack behavior that features excellent illustrations.

Where there are elves,
there are wolves.

No, I'm not neglecting the trolls. Let's talk about blacksmithing and jewelry making. You may be able to meet a blacksmith through a horse farm, through the SCA, at a Renaissance Festival, or at some other site that stages historical reenactments. The last three may offer similar opportunities to let you speak with a jeweler. If none of these options are available, and you need to write about trolls, it's back to the bookshelf. Unfortunately, most modern texts on metalcraft presuppose the use of modern power tools, so we'll have to fudge where necessary. Modern books also tend to focus on toolmaking, not weapons-making. Many of the techniques will be the same, though.

The Practical Handbook of Blacksmithing and Metalworking by Percy M. Blandford is reasonably comprehensive and well-illustrated. The first twelve chapters deal with ironworking, the last seven with metalworking. *Practical Projects for the Blacksmith* by Ted Tucker starts the reader at the forge, is well-illustrated with sketches and photos, and features an excellent glossary of technical terms and a discussion of metallurgy. Alexander G. Weygens' *The Modern Blacksmith* is one of the easiest books for a novice to follow that I've found. Every page is illustrated by the author and the margins bear clearly labelled, step-by-step instructions for the technique currently under discussion. The book also includes a good glossary and clear photographs of tools. Even the back cover is instructive: on it are color photos, showing the hues that steel turns when exposed to different temperatures and heat-treating techniques.

Other books that may be of interest to troll fans are *Working With Metal* by Pamela Tubby, which describes working soft metal (no harder than mild steel); simple jewelry-making questions may be answered in Garrison and Dowd's *Handcrafting Jewelry: Designs and Techniques*, which features sections on casting, stone setting and forging.

Finally, how about the world itself? You won't need to map out the entire world for your holt or campaign, just a small part of it. If you're an absolute tyro of a mapmaker (like me) perhaps you can find what you need in a commercially produced topographic map. *The Essential Whole Earth Catalog* lists two sources of such products: Raisz Landform Maps, 130 Charles Street, Boston MA 02114; and United States Geological Survey topographic maps, information for which may be had by sending a SASE to Map Distribution, US Geological Survey, PO Box 25286, Federal Center Building 41, Denver CO 80225.

There are several general "field guides" available in bookstores. Among these are the Audubon Society Field Guides (16 books as of late 1987), published by Alfred A. Knopf; and the Peterson Field Guides (35 books) published by Houghton Mifflin. These cover a variety of animal and plant life and terrain types, and are illustrated with excellent photos and/or drawings. Select only the books you need.

It is important to remember, however, that **WoTM** exploits do not take place on our Earth; therefore, new and different forms of animal (and plant) life can be introduced as long as they fit into the ecology. (However, be real. There are no unicorns and dragons; no such critters exist on the **WoTM**, by creative decree. Remember?) One place to find what logical extensions of Earth-type creatures might look like is *After Man: a Zoology of the Future* by Dougal Dixon, a comprehensive field guide to one possible future of Earth animal life, with several chapters explaining how and why animal life evolves in response to specific circumstances. The book is fully illustrated in color with fascinating and beautiful drawings; it may even make you a little sad to realize that the animals depicted do not exist...yet.

These books are intended as starting points, no more, for your research. You will doubtless find even more inspiration in your local library or bookstore, or by browsing through a volume such as *The Essential Whole Earth Catalog: Access to Tools and Ideas* (a wellspring of source material!).

In closing, I would like to recommend several old friends that may influence more than your writing of *Elfquest* pastiche. The first is *People of the Lie* by M. Scott Peck. Written by a psychiatrist/minister, this book offers fascinating insights on the evil personality and the possible curing of same. Another resource is an essay by Poul Anderson, "On Thud and Blunder", which was most recently published in Anderson's collection

Fantasy! and is a must-read for any budding fantasy writer. The third is the deceptively small and slender *The Elements of Style* by Strunk and White, a timeless commentary on the art of writing. (Most college courses should be as informative as that single book.)

A final word to those of you who want to write in the world of *Elfquest*: may your illusions be wondrous and unfailing.

A Selected Bibliography

Blacksmithing, Metalcraft and Jewelery Making

Blandford, Percy W.
The Practical Handbook of Blacksmithing and Metalworking
TAB Books, Blue Ridge Summit, PA, 1980.

Garrison, William E. and Dowd, Merle E.
Handcrafting Jewelry: Designs and Techniques
Contemporary Books, Inc., Chicago, IL, 1972.

Tubby, Pamela
Working With Metal
Thomas Y. Crowell, New York, NY, 1972.

Tucker, Ted
Practical Projects for the Blacksmith
Rodale Press, Emmalus, PA, 1980.

Weygens, Alexander G.
The Modern Blacksmith
Van Nostrand Reinhold Co., New York, NY, 1974.

Herb Reference and Natural Dyes

Bemiss, Elijah
The Dyer's Companion
Dover Publications, New York, NY, 1973.

Lust, John
The Herb Book
Bantam Books, New York, NY, 1974

Pahlow, Mannfried
Living Medicine: the Healing Properties of Plants
Thorsons Publishers Ltd., Wellingboro, Northamptonshire, England, 1980.

Weiner, Michael A.
Earth Medicine, Earth Food
Collier Books, New York, NY 1972

Medical Reference

American Red Cross
Standard First Aid and Personal Safety
American Red Cross, 1979.

Berkow, Robert (ed.)
The Merck Manual of Diagnosis and Therapy
Merck and Company, Rahway, NJ, 1982.

Brown, Terry and Hunter, Rob
Concise Book of Outdoor First Aid
Gage Printing, Agincourt, Canada, 1978.

Franks, Martha Ross
The American Medical Association's Handbook of First Aid and Emergency Care
Random House, NY, 1980.

Henderson, John
Emergency Medical Guide
Mc-Graw-Hill, New York, NY, 1978.

Mashiro, N.
Black Medicine: The Dark Art of Death
Paladin Press, Boulder, CO, 1978.

Tegner, Bruce
Self-Defense Nerve Centers and Pressure Points
Thor Publishing Company, Ventura, CA, 1978.

Survival Skills and Everyday Life in the Woods

Angier, Bradford
Survival with Style
Vintage Books/Random House, New York, NY, 1972.

Brown, Tom Jr.
Tom Brown's Field Guide to the Forgotten Wilderness
Berkley Books, New York, NY, 1987.

(with B. Morgan) *Tom Brown's Field Guide to Living with the Earth*
Berkley Books, New York, NY, 1984.

(with B. Morgan) *Tom Brown's Field Guide to Nature Observation and Tracking*
Berkley Books, New York, NY, 1983.

Tom Brown's Field Guide to Wild Edible and Medicinal Plants
Berkley Books, New York, NY, 1985.

(with B. Morgan) *Tom Brown's Field Guide to Wilderness Survival*
Berkley Books, New York, NY, 1983.

(with William Owen) *The Search*
Berkley Books, New York, NY.

(as told to William Jon Watkins) *The Tracker*
Berkley Books, New York, NY.

Boswell, John (ed.)
The U.S. Armed Forces Survival Manual
Rawson, Wade Publishers Inc., New York, NY, 1980.

Graves, Richard
Bushcraft: A Serious Guide to Survival and Camping
Warner Books, New York, NY, 1978.

Olsen, Larry Dean
Outdoor Survival Skills
Pocket Books, New York, NY, 1976.

Weapons Combat

Daniel, Charles
Traditional Ninja Weapons: Fighting Techniques of the Shadow Warrior
Unique Publications, Burbank, CA, 1986.

Demura, Fumio
Bo: Karate Weapon of Self-Defense
Ohara Publications, Burbank, CA, 1976.

Inosanto, Daniel (with George Foon and Gilbert Johnson)
The Filipino Martial Arts, as taught by Dan Inosanto
Know Now Publishing Company, Los Angeles, CA, 1980.

Inosanto, Daniel (with George Foon)
Absorb What Is Useful
Know Now Publishing Company, Los Angeles, CA, 1982.

Williams, John C. (with Glenn Helgeland)
Archery For Beginners
Contemporary Books, Inc., Chicago, IL, 1976.

Yamashita, Tadashi
Bo: The Japanese Long Staff
Unique Publications, Burbank, CA, 1986.

Wolves and Zoology

Dixon, Dougal
After Man: A Zoology of the Future
St. Martin's Press, New York, NY, 1981.

Fox, Michael
The Wolf
Lorgman Canada Ltd., Toronto, Ontario, Canada, 1973.

Lopez, Barry H.
Of Wolves and Men
Charles Scribner's Sons, New York, NY, 1978.

WINNOWILL

WENDY
©85 PINI

From the sketchbook, a "what-if?" — If *Elfquest* were an aquatic adventure,
what would Winnowill be like?

Getting Bent

or: Thinking Like an Elf

by Wendy Pini

The ease of creating an alien race that is humanoid but definitely inhuman is directly proportional to the degree that the aliens deviate from human norms. Even in a crowded subway, a fellow with three eyeballs will tend to stand out — moreso if the eyes are at the end of stalks. This is the easy way to indicate a character's alienness. But when the physical differences between human and alien are very subtle — say, an acceptably normal human appearance that masks infra-red vision and a sense of smell comparable to a bloodhound's — communicating those differences becomes trickier. Even more delicate is the task of revealing the alien emotional and psychological makeup, which must differ in significant ways from the corresponding makeup of a human, and yet be capable of producing "events" identifiable as thoughts and feelings.

The elves of *Elfquest* are not mythological creatures. They are evolved, shape-shifting aliens whose adopted elfin traits breed true because of the high survival rate/value of all who possess those characteristics. The progenitors of this elf-like race, which have been nicknamed the Coneheads, were slender humanoids with elongated limbs and somewhat conical skulls. The Coneheads evolved from humble beginnings, through a period of high technology and space travel, only to return to their biological and spiritual evolution.

The Coneheads discovered and perfected the use of the "magic" which slept within them. Their powers included various forms of psychokinesis, self-mutation down to the genetic level (shape disguise), astral projection, and manipulation of energy fields. It was, by then, a short evolutionary step to the complete abandonment of physical form and resulting existence on a purely cosmic, spiritual plane. But the Coneheads chose not to take that step. They retained their physical bodies, highly mutable though they were, and proceeded to become planet-hopping voyeurs, changing shape to blend in with the creatures on the inhabited worlds they visited.

According to the Scroll of Colors, the history of the High Ones.

All moral judgments aside, the Coneheads were not infallible. The *Elfquest* story is an intimate and detailed chronicle of one of their mistakes and its far-reaching consequences. The earthlike World of Two Moons is our stage. Its indigenous, intelligent inhabitants are, for all practical purposes, human beings and the flora and fauna are only slightly different from those which existed during Earth's prehistory. (Some poetic license has been taken. For example, although most of the animals seen in *Elfquest* resemble their terrestrial Pleistocene counterparts, there are still a few large saurian leftovers from earlier eras. It makes for intrigue.) As revealed in *EQ#20* (*all references here are to the original WaRP editions of the series - Ed.*) the Coneheads had intended to visit the double-mooned planet, disguised as elves, during its fairy lore-minded "middle ages."

But the trolls, servants to the Coneheads, rebelled and caused an accident which hurled the castle-ship back in time to the planet's paleolithic era. The High Ones' (it's at the point when the ship crashes that the Coneheads start to be referred to as the "High Ones") frail, elfin bodies were ill-suited to the harsh environment then prevailing. The atmosphere, for reasons as yet unexplained, had a draining effect on all their "magic" powers. Unable to propel their ship back into space, the High Ones, as elves, were stranded.

The subjects of the *Elfquest* saga, the tribe known as the Wolfriders, are the product of many adaptive changes made by the High Ones and their descendants over untold generations. The Wolfriders exist in their world's mesolithic era. Like the wolf packs they emulate, the Wolfriders hunt and roam the large territory they have claimed; but like certain human tribes they require a "home base" — in this case, the Holt. Over countless turns of the seasons the Wolfriders have had many different holts, but they have lived in their current one (that is, current to the beginning of the EQ tale) since the reign of Goodtree, who founded it.

The Wolfriders haven't much changed their lifestyle since Huntress Skyfire ousted Two-Spear and brought her tribe to an awareness of "the way," a loose code of behavior that stresses harmony with nature. It may safely be assumed that events in *EQ#20* will precipitate irreversible changes in the Wolfriders' attitudes and in the tribal culture (though when and how these changes show up is still *terra incognito*). But Bearclaw dealt with much the same problems and conflicts as did other chiefs before him. Though the Wolfriders have never been a stagnant society, neither have they been truly progressive until Cutter's rule.

Elfquest elves have certain obvious physical traits, the equivalent of the aforementioned three eyeballs, that differentiate then immediately from humans. However, since the story focuses on characterization, it is far more important to examine that indefinable "bentness" which makes elf-think different from human-think. Emotionally, the elves' makeup is similar to ours. The characters laugh, cry, know anger, fear and hatred. But their thought processes are, by human standards, skewed. Their logic goes so far in a straight line and then bends.

Humans tend to think in terms of time. *How long will this take? When do we eat? How long will I live?* We are fully aware of our own mortality and spend most of our lives trying to cram all the living we can into the hours alloted us. The Wolfriders, too, are mortal. But they can live a very long time — several thousand years. Therefore, the line between mortality and immortality is fuzzy at best. But fear of death from any cause is not at the forefront of most Wolfriders' conscious thoughts.

the Wolfrider's view
mortality — then...

...and now.

Whatever sense of urgency they experience is derived from immediate circumstances and not from general angst about a fleeting life span. A Wolfrider will worry about the possibility of dying if there is a sabretooth nearby — he will *not* worry about dying of old age. (Also, general awareness of the Wolfriders' lifespan — which is shorter than that of a pure-blooded elf — did not come until Cutter's time; until then, the tribe pretty much assumed that life was short because death was always premature and unnatural.)

In their emulation of and actual mind-to-mind contact with wolves the Wolfriders have developed a state of consciousness known as "the now of wolf thought." In this state, which when taken to extremes is like a trance, an elf can go about his regular activities with no anticipation of anything beyond the moment, untroubled by hope or fear. The Wolfriders regard it as a practical and desirable way of existence during periods of non-crisis.

While they can communicate telepathically to a certain extent with their wolf friends, the Wolfriders avoid doing it, primarily because lupine body language is so clear in its meaning, and also because a "wolf send" is brain-breaking hard work! When an elf does enter a wolf's mind via telepathy he receives only impressions — the sending between Cutter and Nightrunner is not to be taken literally. Wolves do not think in complete sentences or in anything like a linear pattern.

Elves are capable of cause and effect rationalization, but when confronted with the unknown they tend to be as curious (and often, because of the "now of wolf thought," as short sighted) as wolves. They may attack something too big for them or they may flee from something harmless. Depending on how much time has passed between similar learning experiences, Wolfriders repeat mistakes just as wolves do. They forget quickly.

Probably the most significant area in which elves differ from humans is in their social and sexual interactions. Although they revere their ancestress Timmain in legends, the Wolfriders have no religion and no moral code beyond "they way." Their attitude toward sex goes beyond any "free love" concept since elfin sexual relations cannot be anything but free. Even those who choose monogamy (in its biological, rather than social or religious sense) are free because mutual fulfillment inspires them thus.

The one fly in the idyllic ointment is Recognition, explained in depth elsewhere in this volume. A male and female elf who do not, for some reason, get along with each other might find themselves trapped in this irresistible genetic bond — in which case mating must take place and pregnancy must result. That is what Recognition is for.

Fortunately, Recognized couples have, as all elves do, the advantage of being able to send. It is very hard not to like someone when his/her soul name is revealed and deepest thoughts and feelings are completely open. Deception and manipulation are impossible. And since with elves, liking is just a short step away from loving, nearly all Recognized couples remain close throughout their lives, long after their children have grown and flown. However, since the deep urge of Recognition fades once mating has taken place, the possibility exists that (1) an elf may Recognize a second partner some time after the first Recognition — this may lead to various and intriguing living arrangements; and (2) an elf could conceivably mate with or even Recognize his or her daughter or son many years after the child's birth, since over long times the relative age difference between parent and child all but disappears and genealogical connections are forgotten. This situation, however, would almost always arise only in response to the absolute unavailability of other potential mates.

"Lovemates join for pleasure and lifemates join for life, but Recognition...ahh!" There are some good points to Recognition. Because of the intense spiritual as well as physical communion, the pleasure quotient is higher in the sexual relations of Recognized couples than in lovemates (which, because of sending, is already higher than we poor humans can know — sigh). The term "lifemate" indicates that lovemates have pair-bonded; Recognition is not necessary for lifemating to take place. The pair may or may not opt for monogamy, but it is not a conscious decision based on possessiveness or jealousy. Lifemating is a "marriage" without ceremony or the need for sanction. It can happen any time, even (rarely) between the very young before sexual activity begins. If one member of a lifemated couple Recognizes a third elf, that elf may be incorporated into the bond to make a three-way union, but lifematings are for life and do not break up except under extraordinary circumstances.

Children belong to and are parented by the entire tribe, although the child will not forget who sired and bore him until many hundreds or even thousands of years have passed. Family units share and know each other's soul names. Child abuse is unheard of, as is spoiling and coddling. It is important that "cubs" learn as quickly as possible the laws of nature and the rules of forest survival. Elf children are encouraged to be brave, but taught to be cautious. They are raised with a sense of self worth and are not loaded down with unrealistic parental expectations. They are allowed to be who they are and to develop whatever talents the possess at their own pace. While elfin parents may have certain hopes that the child may be the vessel of one of the "magic" abilities that elves are known to express, there is usually no pressure for the child to "get out

36

there and perform." Redlance's treeshaping powers showed up rather late as such things go; Rainsong knows her cub will be a healer like his grandfather, but does not know how or when the power will mature.

In humans possessiveness, jealousy and the need for control are all products of insecurity. Insecurity stems, in large part, from the inability to communicate with others. Among the Wolfriders, communications is a fine art — the tribe's number is never very large and each member is vital to the survival of the tribe. Within the tribal system there are fights, challenges and disagreements, but once resolved there is no aftermath of resentment. Like wolves, the Wolfriders squabble and then forget it. Unlike wolves, they are not ruthless about picking on "omegas" (low members on the totem pole — which raises the question: *are* there any low members, and if so how are they determined?). Capable of compassion and empathy, the elves do not coldly weed out the weaker or less effectual members of the tribe.

Another aspect of the vastly increased potential for communication afforded by sending is the "soul name," a construct necessitated by the individual's need to maintain *some* part of himself as private. Since it is possible that a telepathic conversation between two elves could leave both minds scoured of those things that make each elf unique, the soul name is a word-sound-concept belonging to (and almost sacred to) each individual. When two or more minds are in telepathic union, each can sense when he is approaching another's soul name and "pull back." Also, each can tell when another is getting close to his own soul name, and each can close off the communication. Only a dark and depraved psyche (like Winnowill) would knowingly invade the mind of another, perhaps even to the point of discovering the soul name. Among Wolfriders, the privacy of thoughts — and especially of soul names — is never questioned.

Ultimately, the key to understanding elf-think (particularly Wolfrider-think) is an awareness of how three factors would affect life as humans know it: a sense of immortality (or lack of a sense of time pressure), an ability to live in the perpetual present, and the ability to communicate intimately with another mind/soul.

Of course, there will always be some for whom elf-think is easier than for others. There is no problem so great it can't be ignored.

37

Portfolio

Being a reprinting, for the first time all in one place, of the portfolio of scenes from Elfquest originally published in 1980 in an edition limited to 1,200 signed and numbered copies, and thus real hard to find now.

The Lure

Blood of Ten Chiefs

Troll King

War - Chieftess

Festival of Flood and Flower

Recognition

Further Conversations
with
WaRP

Volume One of the *Elfquest Gatherum*, which was published in 1981, contained an interview with Wendy and Richard Pini (is there *anyone* left who doesn't yet know that "WaRP," the name of the Pinis' publishing company and general combined persona, is an acronym?). As editor Dwight Decker said then, there's nothing like an interview for getting to know someone in print. Since a lot of water has gone over the dam and under the bridge since then, we felt that an update would not be out of place. However, the comics/publishing/film business has been so very tumultuous during the last seven years, and we discovered that just one interview wouldn't — indeed, couldn't — span the changes WaRP has been through. So we've included two of them! Taken with the Volume One interview, these conversations span the ten year history of Wendy and Richard re: *Elfquest* in about equal thirds.

The first of this pair of interviews took place in late 1984 in Poughkeepsie. The original WaRP *Elfquest* series had recently ended, and the Marvel Comics reprints had yet to start up. Mingled feelings of "postpartum" depression and optimism about new titles and animation ran high. The interview was conducted by Peter Sanderson.

The second interview took place in late 1987 in Philadelphia. The new *Elfquest* tale, *Siege at Blue Mountain*, had been running for about a year, Wendy and Richard had been around the block several times in an effort to turn the story of the Wolfriders into an animated film, and WaRP the company had undergone its own bout of expansion and contraction. The general mood is different, as is the overall state of the comics market. The interview was conducted by John Weber.

PETER SANDERSON: *Do you see* Elfquest's *success as a spur to the creation of more comics in the fantasy genre?*

WENDY PINI: We're surprised that there haven't been more already. *Elfquest* took eight years to be told. And we thought that perhaps we'd see more elves and fairies pop up, but they didn't. I think it's because a lot of creators still don't identify with the genre and would rather do something they're more comfortable with.

RICHARD PINI: It's a notoriously difficult genre to work with because it's so easy to abuse. Even superheroes, by whatever ways they get around them, still pay a kind of homage to the laws of physics and so forth. In fantasy, if you are undisciplined, you can create a world and very quickly get tangled up in its lack of laws, its lack of internally consistent logic. And I think this is probably what scares most people off. It seems very easy, but as soon as most people try it, they find it's very difficult. But again, I think that *Elfquest* has already had some effects on the attempt to do fantasy in comics. I think there are a couple of fantasy comics out there that certainly weren't out there before *Elfquest* and perhaps might have been inspired into existence by *Elfquest*'s success. We had a good laugh over the ads for *Grimwood's Daughter* round about the time *Elfquest* 19 or 20 was coming out. One ad said, "The elves are dying," (Wendy laughs) and no one at Fantagraphics will ever convince me that wasn't a little aside at *Elfquest.*

WENDY: I think an even more astringent aside was "Elves like you've never seen before" (laughter). What, Vulcans? C'mon (laughter)! Punk Vulcans (more laughter)!

RICHARD: Jan Strnad is a fine writer.

WENDY: Yeah.

RICHARD: I've liked everything he's done so far.

WENDY: Jan has soul.

RICHARD: He does have soul. Whether or not *Grimwood's Daughter* is an attempt to come in through the door *Elfquest* has opened, or whether it's absolutely independent — "I have this idea and I've wanted to do it for a long time and it wouldn't have mattered if *Elfquest* had never existed" — I think in some ways you will see more fantasy because of *Elfquest*. But I also think people will discover how difficult it is to do well.

SANDERSON: *Do you think it's necessary to have a personal vision in the work to do fantasy whereas superheroes to some extent can be done by rote?*

WENDY: I think anything good is done with a personal vision, and if anything is done by rote, it's going to show. Any genre, whether it's superhero, western, fantasy, or science fiction, has to have a personal vision to lend it the substance and structure it needs to fly, to continue.

RICHARD: You look at Frank Miller's *Daredevil*. He took a character that was going in seventeen different directions and suddenly stamped upon it in large letters "FRANK MILLER'S VISION", maintained it for the period he was doing it, and then went away. People are trying to follow that lead now and not succeeding nearly as well as Frank did. It's interesting to read, but not the way it was.

WENDY: I think we can go back to the example of *Weirdworld*. Elements were introduced into *Weirdworld* — Black Riders, dragons, elves, wolves — all the things your average fantasy and science fiction reader is accustomed to seeing. These are cliché symbols of fantasy. But in my opinion there wasn't enough of a new twist added onto it to give it any substance. So you had all these wonderful little clichés floating around and nothing to hold it all together, no direction for it to go in. You have to have something to say, no matter what you're doing, and then you pick the symbols with which to say it, because comics is a visual medium as well as a writer's medium. You have to combine the two. Both areas of the medium have to have a vision. You can have terrific artwork, but if the script is soulless and dead, it's going to be felt. You can have a terrific script, but if the artwork is soulless and dead, it's definitely not going to fly.

RICHARD: And if you don't have a vision, you had better be one excellent craftsman, because in a sense you have to fake it, to make it look as if you are very much involved with what you're doing. It's just that the majority of creators can't or don't.

WENDY: And again, you have this steamroller of scheduling, which is that this HAS to be OUT THIS MONTH (laughter), y'know? And when creativity

> "You have to have something to say, no matter what you're doing, and then you pick the symbols with which to say it, because comics is a visual medium as well as a writer's medium."

comes up against something like that, then it becomes a real grind, and my admiration goes out to anyone who can rise above that grind and make a statement the way Frank Miller did.

SANDERSON: *To what extent did* Elfquest *turn out at the end as you saw it at the beginning? Did the plot and characterizations change from what you had originally intended?*

WENDY: Well, our formula for doing *Elfquest* was initially to plot the whole thing out. Even before we did our first promo package back in 1977, we knew how it was going to end.

RICHARD: I have to jump in here with an amendment to that. The overall plot did not change. But you (Wendy) and I had a number of discussions on points. The whole of issue 20, I think, was more vague in our minds at the beginning than it came out being, when we finally got around to putting that issue out.

WENDY: Well, we always knew that the elves were going to reach the castle, and that they were going to discover their origins.

RICHARD: True, but I'm referring particularly to the whole idea of "what does death mean?" So we had to give some thought to and make some decisions about what death and after-death are to these characters. We were faced with a little bit of a dilemma in that we didn't want to say in every case that first death happens, and then *this* happens, because we wanted the readers to think about what things like life and death mean, not only to the characters, but to themselves as readers.

WENDY: I will readily admit that up until issue 19 we debated about whether One-Eye was really dead, or whether we would revive him. Richard loved him and wanted him back, and I felt for the integrity of the story he had to die. And during the course of our debates, we came upon the chilling third alternative, which is only doing justice to the nature of elves, which is not the same as the nature of humans. We established early on in the story that the elves have the capacity for astral projection, that is, the spirit existing outside the body. So why wouldn't it follow, then, that the spirit would continue to be a force after the body has died? And as we began to talk about this more, and realize that death, in our minds, probably isn't the same thing for elves as it might be for humans, we realized we had to deal with this as a story concept, and have the other characters deal with it. Clearbrook calls out to her mate's spirit; the spirit doesn't respond. Usually, in a fantasy story, when someone's love calls out to a spirit, the spirit returns and everyone lives happily ever after. Why didn't this happen in *Elfquest?* Because not only did we want the characters to think about it, but we also wanted the readers to think about it. Maybe dying isn't as bad as we've been led to believe. Maybe death is another state that you don't necessarily want to come back from.

RICHARD: And we weren't about to make that choice, certainly not for the readers. We didn't want to impose whatever feelings we had on them by saying, "The reason One-Eye does not answer Clearbrook is that he's out there in the Elysian Fields having a grand old time with all the other characters who have died." And so, by leaving it

with a big question mark in that respect, I'd like to think we have very subtly forced the readers to think about the concept of living, the concept of dying, the concept of spirit, the concepts of afterlife and nonexistence.

WENDY: It is something that's not really focused on with any kind of consistency in superhero comics. Particularly in the Marvel Universe, resurrection is the rule of the day. If enough readers write in and say, "I miss that character," they'll find some way to bring him back. Therefore, the fans get this idea, "We have the power of life and death over the characters we like; therefore, we shouldn't really take death seriously when it happens in a story."

> "Maybe dying isn't as bad as we've been led to believe. Maybe death is another state that you don't necessarily want to come back from."

RICHARD: They want what they're used to. They don't want to think they have no power over One-Eye. At the World Science Fiction Convention someone said, "When are you going to bring One-Eye back?" And we looked at this person in the audience and said, "One-Eye's story is told. You have to relate to it however you want." And this person sort of sat in his chair and went "Ohhhh...." (Wendy explodes in laughter). And that's the answer we had for them. They have no power over the characters, and therefore, they are getting a more truthful experience in the reading of the story.

SANDERSON: *They are being forced to recognize the reality of death.*

RICHARD: They've been forced all through *Elfquest* to accept the reality of the various and sundry things we've put in there. The reality of death. The reality of...

WENDY: Sex.

RICHARD: Of sex. The reality of love as an emotion and what it means. The reality that you can think differently from the way I think, but that doesn't make you wrong and me right, or vice versa; and we can still get along. I hope it's been a subtle manipulation, but not an unkind one.

WENDY: Let me make a point about the fans which I think is very important. They are often put down by people in the industry because of the tendency they have to say, "This character died, but I want him back," and all that. It is the industry itself that has created the belief in fans that they have that power. If someone says, "No, this is the way it's going to be," I maintain that most fans are intelligent enough and respectful enough to say, "Oh, okay.

Hey, this is something different." And they'll like that. They really like to be treated with respect.

SANDERSON: *You must have felt a great deal of pressure to keep the series going.*

RICHARD: Oh, heavens, we generated a lot of that pressure ourselves. Most of our readers, when they wrote in to comment on issue 20, said, "I am very sad that *Elfquest* is ending; it's been a part of my life. But you did good, you wrapped it up, and I'm happy for the experience and for having known it." We still get letters saying, "Oh please, please, please don't let it end. Please continue." But most people were quite understanding that way. I'm sure in the back of their minds, they kind of hope we'll continue. We even created some of that pressure ourselves. Here we've got the best selling independent comic going at the moment, and we're cutting it off. After eight years of doing the same thing under very intense conditions, it was absolutely necessary that we take a break. We've said repeatedly that the characters are not dead. They're not even in limbo for very long. We have other plans. But they're other plans of ours, and not a response to the pressure coming from outside.

WENDY: In other words, the next *Elfquest* you see will come out when it's time for us to do it, not because there's a lot of screaming. Although, I confess, I hope the screaming continues, because that means the interest will still be there.

RICHARD: If the screaming continues, it will be because of the Marvel reprints, because that incarnation will be the one that bridges the gap as far as comics output is concerned for the next three years.

WENDY: And hopefully, by the end of that three years, we'll also have the film coming out, and when who knows what kind of demand there'll be for *Elfquest?* If the film's a success we've already discussed the possibility of opening up a subgenre of *Elfquest* aimed almost exclusively at children, but with the same kind of quality we've been putting into the adult-oriented *Elfquest.*

RICHARD: It's almost going to be a Star Comics version of *Elfquest* specifically for very young readers.

WENDY: We will leave the controversial stuff out, but not the questions we ask. We want them to think. We just won't deal with certain things.

SANDERSON: *When you speak of new plans*

for Elfquest *in the future, are you talking about new stories?*

RICHARD: Oh, yes.

WENDY: The next thing that will happen will be a graphic novel, which will be a self-contained story.

RICHARD: We're tentatively looking for it to be two years down the line, in autumn 1986, as a hundred-page graphic novel in the color volume *Elfquest* format. It will be a new story that picks up the characters where we left off at the end of issue 20. We deliberately left things unanswered. We knew there were more stories. There will probably be three or four new graphic novels over the next few years.

WENDY: At present I can see only two. The next graphic novel will have everything to do with where we left off. What effect has the knowledge of their origin had on the Wolfriders, these primitive little creatures suddenly confronted with the universe opening up?

RICHARD: We've said for years that *Elfquest* is a novel with twenty chapters. It has a beginning, a middle and and end. True and false. It's completed, it's done, but as Wendy has said, there are other adventures. Ultimately, however, there is an absolute brick-wall ending beyond which there is nothing else. And that is eventually going to show up in a graphic novel, as I say, two or three or four down the line.

WENDY: When Arthur Conan Doyle wanted to kill off Sherlock Holmes, he had done what he could with the character, and he was tired of it. And the fans forced him to bring him back, and it was never the same. That is never going to happen to us.

SANDERSON: *What about the previous generations of the Wolfriders?*

RICHARD: That's the project we're calling *Blood of Ten Chiefs*, which is a shared universe anthology series. For the last several years Bob Asprin and Lynn Abbey have been editing a very successful series of anthologies based on a concept called *Thieves' World*. Bob and I were sitting around one day, and I mentioned to him an idea Wendy and I had for a storybook called *Blood of Ten Chiefs*. There'd be a little story on each one of the chiefs, and Wendy would do illustrations. Bob suggested, "Why don't you have other authors involved in this?" This was an intriguing idea. So for the last six months to a year, we've been getting together all the pieces of paperwork that are necessary. This is a monstrously complicated administrative thing to do. We're at the point now where we have an agent who is making a pitch to publishers for the books,

and we have a list of authors, and the four of us — Wendy and myself, and Bob Asprin and Lynn Abbey — will co-edit. We're very excited about it because it represents an infusion of imagination beyond what we two are able to come up with on our own. It's easy at this point to feel burned out about the characters. But somebody who hasn't been living cheek by jowl with the story for the last eight years can manage to come up with all sorts of new things.

WENDY: We've had to be very careful in how we've guided the other hands that have become involved in the perpetuation of the *Elfquest* mythos. For instance, the Chaosium *Elfquest* role-playing game is doing very well. Of necessity, new additions have had to be made to the *Elfquest* universe; for instance, the concept of Prairie Elves and the concept of Sea Elves, which I myself had never dealt with in the story and never would have dealt with in the story. But for the game it's good to have other characters who can be met along the road. But when the fans write in and say, "Do these also exist in Wendy and Richard's universe?" we have to say a very firm "No." Nothing really exists in *Elfquest* until we put it down on paper ourselves. Also, for the fan fiction that comes in we publish in *Yearnings*. When a series, such as *Star Trek*, stops, fans have a tendency to want to keep it going by doing their own stories and artwork; and eventually,

if the series is long enough away, the fans begin to think of their own fiction as being The Thing. And they get confused. So that's why we're trying to keep as much of a handle as possible on the fan fiction that's done, and to continually keep it in their awareness that this is fan fiction.

SANDERSON: *Will the* Blood of Ten Chiefs *stories be officially part of the canon?*

RICHARD: We are going to be very careful about what goes into *Blood of Ten Chiefs* in terms of making sure it is consistent. I think right now we've come to a decision that it will be part of the *Elfquest* story. We stand behind what these authors will do in *Blood of Ten Chiefs*. We will not stand behind what someone rolls the dice for in the role-playing game or what somebody writes as a piece of fan fiction.

WENDY: When I was a fan, I thought as a fan, I behaved as a fan; but when I became a professional, I put away fannish things (laughter). That's essentially it. We can get behind these professionals; they're top storytellers in their field.

SANDERSON: *Would you allow other writers and artists to deal with the characters in* Elfquest *itself?*

WENDY: Absolutely. In fact, I'm looking forward to the possibility of a collaboration with a young woman who has worked as an animator on the West Coast. She's the first person who has ever given original drawings of my characters to me that have contained facial expressions exactly as I would do them, but not traced. She's got a feeling for the characters like no one else I've encountered. And I'm hoping that perhaps she can become an assistant penciller on the graphic novels, because if everything goes well, for the next three years I'm going to be up to my neck in production of the animated film. And if we have to have a graphic novel out in two years, not all the work can be mine.

RICHARD: I think a general answer to that question would be that aspects of any given project might be given over to others, to a greater or lesser extent. But I can't imagine a creative project that we would simply turn over lock, stock and barrel to some other team of people to write, to create, to draw, to do everything else, without our involvement on some level.

WENDY: That's precisely because of what we were saying about fantasy before. It's too easy for it to get out of control. It's so tempting to say, "Let's haul in a dragon or a unicorn" (laughter). And the more people who become connected to the *Elfquest* universe, I think the more temptation there will be to say, "Let's pull out all the stops. We can do anything. There are no rules."

SANDERSON: *Did simply the fact that* Elfquest *took eight years to do change it in any way?*

WENDY: Yes. I started the series when I was 26 years old, and that was all the living I had done, and now I'm 33, and oh, boy, the living that Richard and I did during those eight years! Really smart readers will watch the relationship between Cutter and Skywise and get an indication of some of our changes in attitude as the story went on, since those are the two characters we identify with the most. I found very early on I identified very strongly with Cutter, but towards the end of the series he

> "It was just a bizarre amalgam of *Elfquest* and *The Wizard of Oz* and *Herself the Elf* and *Peyton Place*...we went back to them and said, 'What is this?'"

became almost too masculine for me to get as close to as he was before. He really grew up. I think it's probably easier for women handling male characters to handle younger characters. But as Cutter matured through the story and asked deeper and deeper questions, I began to step back from him, sort of to retreat into the Kahvi character (laughter) who was a female I could relate to a lot easier than to what Cutter had become. All the characters grew. They all changed. All the characters resolved something in their own hearts. In the first five issues

I don't think that was ever in our minds, the depths to which the characters would go.

RICHARD: There was no need for that at the beginning, because those first issues were establishment, and then let's get on with the quest. As things progressed, we knew we were going to have to deal on a gritty, realistic level with war, with love, with sex, with life, with death. It became necessary to devote more and more space to each of these things because they are inherently complex things. There were times when we wondered, because of things *we* were thinking or feeling, whether a character would do "A" or do "B". We might have planned "A" way back at the beginning, but because of our own growth and our own experiences over years of time, we had to ask is it still reasonable to expect "A" or is this character going to do B?

WENDY: Winnowill was a character who surprised us because the series would have been fifteen issues long if it hadn't been for her. We had originally planned only the fifteen issues. I think issue #11, where she was introduced, was the turning point for the depth of the story to increase. She turned it into a character that I found fascinating. She is so subversive and so subtle in what she does. She never comes out and does violence until the end of her part in the story. Just watching her little spider web break thread by thread became a very fascinating thing. The darker quality of the story began to come out at that point.

SANDERSON: *How did the* Elfquest *animated film project come about?*

RICHARD: It was in 1981, in the fall, that we got a call from the Nelvana studio up in Toronto. They were interested in doing *Elfquest* as a full length animated film, which was our goal. We tried to work with them for almost two years, during which time it became increasingly obvious that these were not easy people to work with, because although their studio was capable of spectacular animation, they did not have a feeling for what 'story' is, how to tell a story. We became more and more frustrated with the things they were trying to tell us should be in the animated film. Then *Rock and Rule* came out and failed, and they decided that animation was not the way to go, and presented us with a treatment of the film that, at the time we received it, we didn't

The Palace of the High Ones — Wendy style...

...and Nelvana style.

know was meant for live action. It was just a bizarre amalgam of *Elfquest* and *The Wizard of Oz* and *Herself the Elf* and *Peyton Place*. When we went back to them and said, "What is this?" they said, "Oh well, we want to do it live action." I said, "Say what?!"

WENDY: I got on the phone with one of the directors and said, "We've got four-foot elves who ride wolves. How do you propose to do that?" And he said, "We'll put children in costumes on trained wolves," which shows how much he knew about wolves.

RICHARD: So, anyway, it took us another several months after that to get the property back. It was under option, and we had to acquire it back legally, and we did. We went looking for another studio. We had done our homework, and decided we didn't want any of the big animation studios — Disney, Bluth, Filmation, Hanna-Barbera, Ruby-Spears, Rankin-Bass — we just didn't want any of them to do it. We didn't like their style of work. So we focused on smaller studios and found a smaller studio on the East Coast, and they turned out not to be as businesslike as we would have liked. So by a great stroke of luck we connected up with a number of people over the last seven or eight months

"...Richard is going Where No Richard Pini Has Ever Gone Before...he taught himself to be a publisher and editor, and now he's teaching himself to be a movie mogul."

who were able to allow us to consider the absurd alternative of starting our own studio. Fortunately, somewhere in there, it was suggested that maybe we'd want to approach an animation studio that's already established, but that we'd raise the funding for the production, have it in hand, and approach a studio from that position of power. Hold the purse strings and you have control over your project. So in essence that is what we have been doing for the last several months. We are working as closely as we can with a studio down in New York City. We are still in the process of acquiring the financing, and should have that tied up within a couple of months, at which point Wendy goes on staff to that studio as creative director, designer of animation, and six other things, because she's the Source.

WENDY: We're also working from a screenplay which probably won't (laughter) remain intact, but at least it's a structure to work from.

SANDERSON: *You expect someone will rewrite the screenplay?*

WENDY: No, I expect we'll have a story conference in which the key animators and the directors get together and from the basic structure we will pick the thing apart and find out what will work cinematically and what won't. That's a process that could take up to eight months.

RICHARD: So Wendy goes on staff with them. I become — in essence if not in fact — what you would call executive producer, because I will be shepherding, as I have done with the *Elfquest* comic, the business aspects and the financial aspects of the film, and she is shepherding the creative aspects of the film.

WENDY: The whole thing is suddenly on a much larger scale. This is national and international. I am looking forward to it and I cannot wait to get to work on this film. It's just going to be the next step, and one that we've been hoping for for so long.

RICHARD: And something else: despite any statements to the contrary, when *Elfquest* was optioned three years ago, that was the first instance I know of a studio optioning an independently owned and creator-controlled comic book series.

WENDY: Unless you count Richard Corben's *Neverwhere*. That appeared in the *Heavy Metal* movie.

RICHARD: That's true. The reason I mention this is the news releases saying that *The DNAgents* being optioned for TV represents a breakthrough for creator-owned comics and creative control over the product — but we were there three years ago. And in fact it was our exercise of our creative control that caused us to leave Nelvana.

SANDERSON: *What is the studio you're now working with?*

RICHARD: The studio is Zander's Animation Parlor. They have done many animated commercials. They also did the CBS-TV special *Gnomes*.

SANDERSON: *Jack Zander used to work on Tom and Jerry at MGM in the 1940s.*

WENDY: He'd be very pleased that you know that. He thinks that nobody knows what he used to do (laughter). I hasten to point out for any of the readers who have seen *Gnomes* that that's not the kind of animation that will be in the *Elfquest* film. If everything goes through as planned, there will be a look to the *Elfquest* film that hasn't ever been seen in an animated feature film before, because the coloring will be done at a studio in Brazil, where they do some spectacularly good airbrush effects. They intend to airbrush each cel, where it's appropriate, so you will have a roundness and a fullness to the figures that has never been seen before.

SANDERSON: *I take it this will be full animation.*

WENDY: Absolutely. No rotoscoping. This is a real cartoon. We are not trying to imitate or to mimic live action. We are trying to create movement on a fantasy level, larger than life.

RICHARD: So that's what's happening with the animation, and it's tremendously exciting for me because it involves talking with people on a level that very few people on the creative end of things get to do in comics.

WENDY: Yes, it's not every day you get to call up Roy Disney (explosion of laughter).

RICHARD: He's one of the individuals we have had to speak to in the past with regard to trying to set up distribution and so forth and so on of a film. And there is marketing, there is publicity, there is licensing, there is a myriad of ancillary things connected with making a film.

WENDY: My part of the film will be essentially what I'm accustomed to, but Richard is going Where No Richard Pini Has Ever Gone Before, and it amazes me how he's holding up through this. Again, he's doing what he's done before: he taught himself to be a publisher and editor, and now he's teaching himself to be a movie mogul (laughter).

SANDERSON: *How much of the story will the film cover?*

WENDY: It will cover the quest proper, from issue 6 through issue 20.

RICHARD: That section of *Elfquest* is a good adventure story. It will need to be pared down tremendously. Certain things will need to be condensed or whatever, but it will survive as a rollicking good adventure story with the values of *Elfquest* intact.

WENDY: What may shake fans of *Elfquest* up a little bit is that events in the story have been condensed, squashed. Certain scenes just won't be in there because cinematically they don't work; they drag. Some characters will be eliminated.

SANDERSON: *Because of time limitations in the film.*

WENDY: Exactly. The animators are going to have to move seventeen Wolfriders through the story, which means that rather than having the tribe constantly on screen, we're going to be focusing on individual characters. For an animated film, it's still going to be a very rich and complex story. The approach that Zander's studio wants to take is to aim at an older child-level family audience. I suppose you could call it around the level of PG-13. They really take the story seriously. They want to tell a story that's going to be talked about both in the sense of filmic storytelling and cinematic inventiveness.

SANDERSON: *How did you get into publishing other people's comics?*

RICHARD: Well, round about issue 14 of *Elfquest*, I was at a convention. I was shown a portfolio of artwork by Colleen Doran, who is doing *A Distant Soil*. I said, "This is very nice; send me some xeroxes." And the next year at the convention I saw her portfolio again, and there was more artwork, and there were sample comic pages. I said, "This looks like it belongs to a story," and I asked her to tell me the story. By the time issue 17 of *Elfquest* had come out and it was very much on my mind that in a year I was going to be a publisher with nothing to publish, because *Elfquest* would be done. So I asked Doran if she'd like to do a book in the *Elfquest* format, and she said yes, and we worked out a contract. Then *Mythadventures* came along in a conversation with Bob Asprin. We were sitting around at a table at yet another convention, and he was expressing a desire to see his books translated into comics form, and it began to appear to me that properties were sort of floating my way. This takes us up to just within the last year. We've started to expand in the sense of gaining new personnel. I'm trying to build a support staff of people. It occurred to me that two titles or three titles is still not very much of a comics publishing company. And it's not that I want to go into the ring and slug it out with First or Eclipse; I just want to be a presence in the independent publishing market. We were a presence with *Elfquest* because *Elfquest* was such a phenomenon. But now it appears to become necessary to act like every other company: have five, six or seven titles that come out on a regular basis, monthly or bimonthly. No more of this three or four months in between because it takes a very special book like *Elfquest* to maintain the interest necessary to wait four months for the next issue. That's where we are right now: we've got *A Distant Soil*, we've got *Mythadventures*, we've got *Thunderbunny*, we've got three or four other titles under consideration, and I would like by the middle of this year to have those half dozen titles coming out bimonthly.

WENDY: But you're branching out into other things as well.

RICHARD: Yeah. We're branching out into

doing books. I intend by the middle of next year to have at least two "book books" under WaRP Graphics' belt. One of them will be an art book on the work of Alex Schomburg, a wonderful man: all his comics covers for Timely and all his science fiction artwork. And the other one will be a book of Wendy's artwork that she did for a project based on the Michael Moorcock fantasy novel *Stormbringer*.

SANDERSON: *You (Wendy) said in the previous* Journal *interview that you couldn't see yourself working in a big corporation.*

WENDY: I was thinking of Marvel. Quite frankly, I couldn't see myself doing that on a regular basis.

RICHARD: It's a different work environment. It's a different pressure environment. Yes, WaRP Graphics is expanding, and in the next year or two,

Two scenes from *Law and Chaos*.

55

three, five, we may take on another two, three or five employees. I think of all the independent comics companies, First Comics is the one that people look at when they want an example of how something is being run well. And I've been to their offices, and I think they have fewer than ten people there. I don't get any impression of *quote* large corporation *unquote* about First Comics. It's still very comfortable. And I think we would be able to maintain that situation so that neither of us nor anyone working for us would feel "I'm a cog in the big machine." I'm very cautious about WaRP Graphics' plans for growth and expansion because I've seen how one can grow too fast, and I don't want that to happen.

WENDY: It's not so much growing fast as over-extending yourself.

SANDERSON: *Do you two see yourselves as staying in comics indefinitely?*

WENDY: I'm still committed to trying to explore the extent of what I'm capable of doing, and that will probably take the rest of my life. Now that *Elfquest* is done, and I've admitted in public I'm elfed out for a while, I want to teach myself how to draw all over again, because having been a cartoonist for eight years, my sense of proportion is all skewed, and whenever possible lately I've been drawing and sketching from life. Cartooning is caricature, but you have to understand the rules before you can break them; and I'm sort of losing my grip on the rules, and I want to go back and find out what the rules are. That's why I want to paint and draw more. That ambition still remains: to paint, to draw, to be a serious artist.

RICHARD: If Wendy is a creative talent, I seem to be an exploitative talent (muffled burst of laughter from Wendy). And I say that with a certain pride because it's necessary. It took both of us to get *Elfquest* going and to make it grow, and I find I enjoy the role of facilitator, if you will, very much. It's what I am going to be doing with respect to the movie; what to whatever extent the other comics and book properties will allow me to do, I will do with them. The concept of finding the right market, or finding the right person to talk to, or finding the glue that holds two pieces of something together, of making it work — the phrase that is put in quotation marks all the time is "wheeling and dealing." That's what I like doing, and I think I'll be doing it for a long, long time.

From Wendy's sketchbook — something *not* Elfquest.

The conversation continues — three years later...

JOHN WEBER: *Tell me, first, how you guys met. It's a great story!*

WENDY PINI: Well, let's see — you told it last time.

RICHARD PINI: I told it last time.

WEBER: *Whose turn is it?*

WENDY: It's my turn this time. This is such an oft-told story, it's become apocryphal by now. As teenagers, we both read and collected comics, specifically Marvel Comics, and...let's see, I guess I was about 18, a senior in high school, and I wrote a letter in to the *Silver Surfer* comic. And, much to my surprise, they published it, along with my address. So I started receiving letters from all over the country, from boys who were interested in meeting a *girl* who read comics (laughter) because back at that time...

WEBER: *It was* Millie the Model, *that's what girls were reading.*

RICHARD: Well, also, there weren't that many female fans, and that there was was a rare and wonderful thing.

WENDY: Conventions were just starting to get off the ground, and everything. Back in the late Sixties, the situation was really primitive (laughter) compared to now. So, as I said, I got letters from all over, and one of these letters really intrigued me because, rather than telling me everything about himself, the writer said, "If you want to know more about me, you have to write me," and that was a letter from Richard Pini at MIT. I got curious, so I wrote, and he wrote, and I wrote, and he called, and I called, and we exchanged photos, and I sent him some drawings, and he sent me some of his writing. We got to know each other, and by the end of that year (1969) we were pretty well certain that this was *it.* We tried to meet off and on in the next four years, while he was finishing college.

RICHARD: From my point of view: I was 19, and

I was hauling my load of comics back home to my dorm room every week, and I was reading this issue, and I was struck by the letter. It was a wonderful letter, it would have been a wonderful letter no matter who wrote it. But the fact that it was by a *female* was doubly enticing (laughter) so I was motivated on two levels to respond, the intellectual and the hormonal. And we saw each other about once a year for the next four years. Those were our "dates".

WENDY: They were very intense dates!

RICHARD: And then, finally, in 1972, I graduated and Wendy moved east. We got married.

WEBER: *Did you meet halfway, in the middle of the country?*

RICHARD: Oh, no. I wrote that first letter in January of 1969, and by August, we pretty much knew we wanted to meet each other. So she was enrolling at a school in Los Angeles, and I was at MIT in Boston. I got into a little Renault and, sixty hours later, I was getting out of the car in Los Angeles.

WENDY: He didn't eat, he lived on Vivarin and Life Savers, and he went straight across the country!

WEBER: *We're lucky you're here today.*

RICHARD: Yes, yesss. I never even saw the town of East Winslow, Arizona, where I got stopped for speeding (laughter).

WENDY: Eighty miles an hour through a town that he didn't see! So...yes, he arrived at my college, and I came out of my dorm room, and there he was down at the end of the hallway, and we sort of did a Clairol ad (laughter), slow-motion towards each other, we recognized each other, and the rest is history.

> "...the fact that (the letter) was by a female was doubly enticing so I was motivated on two levels to respond, intellectual and hormonal...we saw each other once a year for the next four years."

WEBER: *So some Marvel editor out there somewhere is responsible for all this?*

WENDY: Marvel Comics takes full credit for it. In fact, we were used as characters in the *Ghost Rider* comic book written by Tony Isabella some years back, which means that Marvel Comics owns us as copyrighted characters. Therefore, we cannot reproduce without Marvel's permission (laughter)!

RICHARD: I don't know, I just dread having to ask permission.

WEBER: *It could be a great legal case. Front page of the* National Enquirer, *I think! Anyway, let's talk*

Art imitates life — sort of. The creators of Elfquest host the Ghost Rider. © 1975 Marvel Comics.

about Elfquest *and the whole notion of it. You had the idea way back when in some form —*

RICHARD: Wendy's always been a storyteller. She's always had pictures and words going around up there. I guess the ingredients of *Elfquest* have been in her mind for a long, long time.

WENDY: In one form or another, the characters have always existed. My cartooning style is highly influenced by Japanese comic books, which I discovered in my early teens. As I began to develop my cartooning style, the characters began to take on more solid form and began to seem more like themselves. I've always drawn little elfin cartoonish figures. In 1977, the time seemed right to bring the book out.

RICHARD: 1977 was a watershed year for all of us in science fiction, fantasy and comics because of *Star Wars.*

WEBER: *How tough was it in the beginning?*

WENDY: Not as tough as it is now.

RICHARD: Back then, there was almost no independent comics market.

WENDY: There were only about three hundred direct sales shops.

RICHARD: Well, we don't even know what the number was. It was a small number compared to now. There was almost no direct sales market. There were only two distributors, Bud Plant, Inc. and Seagate Distributors, distributing to this fledg-

ling market. That's all there was. We started out with a loan from my parents, not knowing how to publish, not knowing where to go, going to the Yellow Pages and looking for a printer because there was not the network of information that there is today. We printed up ten thousand copies of *Elfquest*, and then went to Bud Plant and Phil Seuling and said, "Will you take our print run?". They said yes, and the rest is history. But, because we were about the only kids on the block with a comic — *Elfquest* — at that time, acceptance was very easy. There was no competing product. Nowadays, my god! You have to have the hide of a rhino to get into this pool!

WENDY: It's not necessarily any harder now to get your product accepted if it is a really exciting new concept, or if it really grabs people in some way. And there are people starting out just exactly the way we did. What comes to mind right now is *Teenage Mutant Ninja Turtles.* They (Eastman and Laird) started out exactly the way we did. They decided to publish it themselves, went through the Yellow Pages and looked up a printer, and it just took off from there. So history does repeat itself, certainly. I think the great difficulty now is in having staying power. Distributors are on very shaky ground right now; they're dropping like flies. Retailers are also losing their stores, and nobody's paying anybody adequately. And everybody's in debt to everybody. So having the ability to hang in there are get your series past four or five issues is very, very difficult.

RICHARD: There's a problem in that a lot of small publishers seem to be looking at things in a skewed way. Some of these publishers may be young kids who are still living at home. They don't have to pay rent, they don't have to buy their own food. They don't have the expenses of a business. So they might feel fine that they're selling two thousand copies of their magazine. They think they're a success. By that standard, I suppose they are. By the standards of the wider industry, that's not true. That same product, to a larger publisher, would be a failure, because it wouldn't be carrying its own weight. It's been a complex, bizarre market for the last year and a half.

WENDY: Yeah, I think it's only just now beginning to start to steady itself. In that steadying, I think we will see a lot of dropping away of the get-rich-quick efforts that have popped up in the past couple of years, and the titles that do have the staying power are the ones that we're going to see continue on the stands.

> "That term, 'hook,' is a deadly one to me. I'd like to throw it up and skeet-shoot it!"

WEBER: *Comics have, I guess in the last year or two, really entered the mainstream, I think, what with the* Superman *revamping,* Dark Knight, *things like that, that are being publicized in the national press.* Waldenbooks *is carrying —*

WENDY: Well, the reason Waldenbooks carries graphic novels at all is because of *Elfquest. Elfquest* was the first graphic novel to be accepted and —

RICHARD: To penetrate that market.

WENDY: In this country.

RICHARD: In a certain sense, you're right. *Dark Knight*, the *Superman* revamp, the *Watchmen* collection, these are all PR coups. Warner Communications went out and they got a lot of interviews in magazines and papers like *Rolling Stone* and *The New York Times*, and TV shows, and so on and so forth. That's still superficial. Comics are still looked at in this country as children's literature, even though you will find *Rolling Stone* talking about the hard grittiness of *Dark Knight*, or whatever. Until there is a section in the Waldenbooks store, for example, devoted to graphic novels — right now, there are probably only three or four, maybe a half dozen graphic novels worthy of the name available — until you have a section of these things that people will go into and browse the way they browse the romances, the way they browse the mysteries, the way they browse science fiction, comics are not yet mainstream.

WENDY: But I agree with you that they are beginning to edge their way in.

WEBER: *What drives me crazy is that, every time you see an outside article on, say, the Batman character, you see the* **Zap, Pow, Boom** *sound effects in the headline. I don't think I've seen a mainstream article that didn't do that.*

WENDY: Well, there's a tremendous amount of inertia, as Richard pointed out, in the way comic books are looked at in this country, and the Zap Pow Boom catches attention, and it's been used for years to immediately associate the audience's thinking with comic books, and, of course, that's not what *Dark Knight* and some of the other things are all about now. There is just an incredible lumbering slowness in changing people's thinking about comics.

RICHARD: There's another thing, and it's very subtle, I think. You're *not* seeing Pow Zap Crash with *Dark Knight* and *Electra: Assassin* and *Watchmen.*

WENDY: Or *Elfquest*, really.

RICHARD: But what you *are* seeing with those other ones is, *"These are the New, Dark, Gritty, Nihilistic Comics for Armageddon, Comics for Adults."* It's a different kind of Pow Crash Bam, and it is, in its way, just as bogus. Because it's a PR hook. It's not really a reality yet. It's a hook, it's a label, it's a pigeonhole.

WENDY: That term, "hook", is a deadly one to me. I'd like to throw it up and skeet-shoot it! "Hook" is a term we hear quite frequently, in terms of marketing a property to the mainstream, and we heard it in the context of *Elfquest* in trying to deal with CBS last year. They had trouble finding a "hook" for *Elfquest*, they had trouble pigeonholing it as a boys' show, a boys' action show, or a girls' fluffy-cute show. *What age group is this aimed at?* they asked. We kept saying this is for everybody, everybody can get something out of it. And they were not able to deal with that concept.

RICHARD: You don't have hooks for mysteries, or cookbooks, unless it's a gimmick book, or romances. They're there! They're part of the literary foundation, or brickwork, or whatever, of this culture. What we need is to have comics become one of those bricks.

WEBER: *Do you think it can happen?*

RICHARD: I think it's got to! It has happened in Japan. It has happened in Europe. There is not the perception in those countries of comics as "kiddie literature", said with a sneer.

WENDY: But I hope what happens in this country doesn't happen like what has happened in Japan, in the sense that, because of the overcrowding of the society, people tend to do a lot of living through the comics. They do their little beehive routine, going to work every day, and getting home, and it takes them two hours to get to work and two hours to get home. Of course, we have that here, too. But once they get home, to a very small apartment in which a family of twelve is living or something, they live through the adventures in the comic books. Out of that, you get comics like *Rapeman* and stuff with incredible violence in it that, I suppose, gets all the day's troubles out of the reader in a catharsis. But I certainly hope that it never goes that far in this country.

RICHARD: But again, I think comics need to become widely accepted as a kind of literature, unless comics want to stay stuck in this little hundred thousand, two hundred thousand, maybe five hundred thousand readership, this tiny little cubbyhole. That's really all the comics fans/readers there are in this country. Whereas you have a lot more people reading John D. McDonald or, God help us, Barbara Cartland.

WENDY: Or L. Ron Hubbard.

RICHARD: Or L. Ron Hubbard (laughter). Well, science fiction has managed to become more mainstream. You find it on the *New York Times* Best Seller list with fair regularity.

WENDY: Since the mid-1970s it's become very respectable because it makes money. Anything that makes money is very respectable in this country.

WEBER: *It's the bottom line, for any business.*

WENDY: Right.

WEBER: *Marv Wolfman, in the introduction to the first volume of* Elfquest, *writes that he envies both of you because you can do whatever you want with the characters, you created them, you publish them. But the more successful* Elfquest *gets, I imagine there's more pressure to keep a certain status quo or to get conservative.*

WENDY: No, at least not in the very seminal part of the book as we publish it. Currently, we're doing the *Siege at Blue Mountain* series, which is done in the same way that we did the original twenty-issue series. We're publishing it in black-and-white first ourselves. Then we'll be going on to collect it into two color volumes, just as the other color volumes were. And *Siege at Blue Mountain* has absolutely no input into it whatsoever but Richard's and mine. We're taking the characters exactly where we want to take them. We get outraged letters from fans who

What *hath* ten years wrought?

don't like the direction that we're taking them, or we get highly encouraging letters from people who like what we're doing and want to see more. We don't care either way. The story's ours. We're taking the characters where they have to go right now. Yes, we still have that luxury.

RICHARD: On the other hand, you have raised a good point: the demand for *Elfquest*. Our readers are very voracious. They are very hungry. Wendy and I — particularly Wendy, because she is the artist, she is the goose that lays the golden eggs — can only do so much in a given period of time, and no more.

WENDY: I like how you put that.

RICHARD: To ask for more is to kill the goose. Nonetheless, we have made the decision that *Elfquest* is large enough, it is a large enough universe and a large enough concept to admit other stories.

WENDY: Absolutely.

RICHARD: And if we can have those stories done in a way that makes us comfortable, if they're good and we're happy with them, then, yeah, we do want to produce them, and it raises the task of having to get other people to produce them. That's why, for example, we have the *Blood of Ten Chiefs* anthology series. These are short stories, prose stories, written by other well-known science fiction people like C.J. Cherryh and Piers Anthony and Robert Asprin and Lynn Abbey. There's a goodly long list! We are in close contact with all of these people, and they are writing about characters in the past. FIrst of all, these characters don't directly intrude upon what we're doing. And they're also characters about which Wendy and I can't really write because we don't have the time we'd like, we don't have all the ideas in our minds that we'd like to express that these other people do. It's fresh material. It's a new way of looking at *Elfquest*, and we're very excited about that. But it does require that we look elsewhere if we want *Elfquest* to grow beyond what two people are physically and creatively capable of doing.

WENDY: I had an interesting conversation with a couple the other day at a convention. The husband asked me, "Doesn't it bother you the way the

> "I don't want to sound judgmental, but we and the ones who have lasted and the ones who are good have paid a certain amount of dues...A lot of the kids who are (self-publishing) now haven't yet. There are very valuable things to be learned in the process of paying dues."

fans trivialize your characters in their own writings and drawings? Doesn't it frustrate you?" He pointed out that their ideas don't seem to be very innovative, that they seem to be very imitative and they're not using their imaginations as much as they could. And I felt compelled to remind him that these were very young people who hadn't done a lot of living yet! There wasn't a lot of life experience to draw on, so much of their experience comes from reading other people's stuff and getting inspired by that. But, moreover, the fact that they're out there doing anything at all, the fact that they're using all of that creative energy for something besides shooting up dope or bashing each other's brains in, I think, is fabulous. I would do anything to encourage that. And possibly, out of that, can grow some people who can actually and truly contribute to the *Elfquest* mythos someday.

RICHARD: Or not even to the *Elfquest* mythos. Let's say that there's a thousand kids out there who are writing, you know, what to us would be juvenile or trivialized stories. Maybe fifty or ten or five or whatever of those will decide that they like writing so much that they're going to keep on writing, so they will keep on writing, they will practice, they will hone their talent and skill and become writers.

WENDY: Really, we both came up through the ranks of fanzines and mimeograph and stencil. Our first exposure to having people read our work and comment on it came through fanzines, and I still think that's a very healthy way to go. But, you know, an ironic thing right now is that I think many fans have been trained through peer pressure to look down on fanzines because of all these little basement publishers who are able to do five hundred issues of *Frogman Versus the Tree Giants*, or whatever, and the distributors BUY THEM (laughter)! So, very often, stuff that is of fanzine or lower quality ends up on the stands, so that important intermediary learning ground of the mimeograph and the little low circulation fanzine is lost.

RICHARD: And the criticism of your peers, even though you may not look at them as that, is gone. You miss the interaction of working with a bunch of

people on a fanzine. Whereas if you sit and do your own comic, you tend to think, "Wow, I'm right up there along with *Elfquest* and any other professionally produced independent comic," and it's a false comparison. I don't want to sound judgmental, but we and the ones who have lasted and the ones who are good have paid a certain amount of dues. A lot of the kids who are doing it now haven't yet. There are very valuable things to be learned in the process of paying dues.

WENDY: Yeah, I think greed has propelled a lot of these kids faster than they really should be going, you know, and the greed of the — well, I won't be all that specific, just greed in general has started a vicious circle in motion. Properties that really aren't well developed have been put out there on the stands. The consumers see the comic on the stands, and it might be the first issue, so they buy it anyway, even though it's junk, and they sock it away —

WEBER: *And they sell it at a convention for ten dollars because it's a first issue.*

RICHARD: Or more often, the dealer, the retailer, buys a bunch of these, hoping, in a month or two, to sell them for ten dollars each, and finds he's not able to do so. So he's stuck with this inventory that he's either paid for or not paid for, but he can't sell it. If he hasn't paid his distributor for it yet, he's not likely to. The distributor has lost that revenue, so, perhaps, he doesn't pay the publisher. And it

becomes a vicious, dirty circle. And everybody hurts. There's an amazing lack of business professionalism in the direct comic sales market. And that is one thing that's got to change. Along with the public perception of comics in this country.

WEBER: *Another problem, with something like Teenage Mutant Ninja Turtles, is that given all of the variations of that title, the original gets pegged in with the imitators. It all becomes distasteful, imitative. You can tell by comparing quality, but if they're all lined up there in one row...*

RICHARD: Somebody who doesn't know, but who has only heard that there are a dozen adjective-adjective-adjective-noun titles won't pick up the *Turtles* because that person doesn't know that this was the precursor, this one has quality. And that's bad. The ones that deserve to die will die, but the ones that deserve to live can be hurt.

WENDY: Even *Elfquest* has run into that, in terms of parodies that have been done over the years, and you know, our characters have been lumped in with the Smurfs and so forth, and it's a complete misconception of the type of fantasy that we're doing. Fantasy itself is very, very difficult to do as a sustained series in comic book form. And I really don't think, apart from *Elfquest*, it's been done in another series that has lasted as long. Fantasy really is such a personal, subjective thing that you have to be able to sustain your vision and your commitment to it over a very long period of time. That's awfully hard to do, especially in the mainstream comics, where the pressure is on to either have a blockbuster, or it's out. With *Elfquest*, we were very lucky. We started at a time when it was possible for us to grow from humble beginnings, and to build a following, an extremely loyal following, so that we were able to stop in 1984, at the peak of *Elfquest*'s popularity, for which we were told by any number of people that we were absolutely insane. And we were able to pick up again in 1986 right where we left off and our readership followed right along with us, and the people that we used to know who read the original twenty issues are now reading *Siege at Blue Mountain*. But it was our ability to sustain the vision and keep our commitment to *Elfquest*, I think, that keeps the fantasy whole. Because we really haven't been bullied by the pressure of sales or the Comics Code or any of the things that many other creators have to deal with.

WEBER: *You talked about* Elfquest *getting too big for two people, and maybe having other people handle it at some point. I read in the* Elfquest Gatherum *(Volume One - Ed.) the review by Paula O'Keefe about the personal involvement and how that makes* Elfquest *work, personal involvement between the two of you, the characters and you two, the characters and the readers. Can that be maintained?*

WENDY: To varying degrees, it can. Certainly we've had our high and low periods of interest in *Elfquest*. Certainly, there have been times when it seemed that it was dominating our lives. We had to take a breather from it for a while, as I did in 1984. For two years, I really didn't do that much with it. We were talking about this in the car on the way here, as a matter of fact. The fact that *Elfquest* does have a life of its own. It does now exist in the great "out there" apart from us, in some ways. It continues to be carried along by its own momentum. We just feel that we are the guiding spirits behind *Elfquest* now. The vision is ours, and whoever handles it, whether it be in animation or when we start up a juvenile line of *Elfquest* stories aimed specifically at a younger audience — we'll have other writers and artists working on that — we will still be where the buck stops. And that's how the story will maintain its integrity and how the characters will not go afield.

RICHARD: You might have asked the same question of Walt Disney. He started back in the 1920s, I think, in his garage, and he was drawing cartoons. Now Walt Disney Productions became a big company, and it produced some mighty fine films. There was always — whatever Disney was like as a person — there was always the Disney stamp. We talk about it today, how it's missing. We look fondly back at *Snow White* and *Pinocchio* and *Sleeping Beauty* and all of that, and we say they're not doing it like that any more. So it *was* possible for a singular vision to either infect or affect a lot of other people who could carry that vision through while one person or two people oversaw it. And we think the same thing is possible now. Maybe the world has changed a little bit, and maybe things are more complex today than they were thirty or forty years ago. But we believe very strongly that the same sort of thing is possible.

WENDY: For instance, we've never lost our belief that, eventually, and hopefully within a very short period of time, we will connect up with a production company and an animation studio that will cooperate with us and give us the kind of creative control that will make us feel comfortable. Certainly, in working to make a film, there comes a point where the studio has to feel that the project belongs to it. They have to feel like the parent and that this is their child. Otherwise, they can't be committed to it. And we firmly believe that we are going to be able to find such a unit that respects our vision and SHARES it, and then can run with it. The search has been a long one, we've been looking for about six years now, and we've been connected up with this studio and that studio. In each case, the problem has been that they've wanted to take the creative control away from us, and to tell the story their way. Rankin/Bass would have done *Thunderelves.* Nelvana would have done a combination of *The Wizard of Oz* and *Rock and Rule* (laughter). This we found out as we worked with them and listened to their version of *Elfquest.* But we know that somewhere out there (Wendy suddenly sings "Somewhere Out There" from *An American Tail*) — and it may be (Don) Bluth, who knows (laughter)? — is the someone who appreciates that *Elfquest* would not have been the success it was but that we made it so. We

> "There's one underlying, fundamental, rock-bottom problem with (animation) — whether it's done in Japan, Los Angeles, New York, or Poughkeepsie. Money."

created it and it went its way with our vision and that's what made it the success it was, and there'll be someone out there who will respect that.

WEBER: *You took the first step — you created it and published it and took care of it for ten years. You ever thinking of taking it the next step yourselves?*

RICHARD: Oh, yeah (laughter)! We got as far at one point in this "filmquest" — we got as far as scouting out locations in the Poughkeepsie, New York area to locate and build an animation studio. We were looking at buildings. There's one underlying, fundamental, rock bottom problem with all of it — whether it's done in Japan, whether it's done in Los Angeles, whether it's done in New York City or whether it's done in Poughkeepsie. Money (laughter). Whether you're gonna build a studio and hire people, or whether you're going to hire an existing studio, or whether you're going to guarantee something, you need *mucho dinero*. For an animated *Elfquest*, we've had different people say different things to us, but let's just say we need anywhere from five to ten million dollars to do a production correctly.

WENDY: Yeah, that's not even as much as some of the films that are out now have cost. *The Black Cauldron* cost 25 million dollars. It was a total bomb. They could have fed Ethiopia with that.

RICHARD: It's kind of obscene when you think about it. But that money has to come from somewhere, whether it's a bank, an investor, a toy company, a studio, which then, for its investment, wants to own the property. A distribution company who, in return for its investment, wants to be able to have input into the making of the movie. It's very convoluted. And what we have seen before us, and what we see before us, is many, many different paths. It's like a spider web - you can go down many strands, and, at different points, there are crossed strands, and you can cross from one path to another, depending upon what you think is the right thing to do. And so, we're staring down these glistening strands of pathways, and working every day, following leads, talking to people, and about the only thing we know is that it's going to happen someday. *Elfquest* could be a Saturday morning series, it could be an afternoon cartoon series, it could be a prime-time special, it could be a prime-time miniseries, it could be a theatrical film, it could be so much, and we're pursuing all of it.

WEBER: *Is it a problem sometimes, your being involved with the characters, being too close to them? Does it handcuff you sometimes?*

WENDY: No, not any more. It used to be, particularly when we were getting towards the end of the series in 1984. That's all our lives were about at that time. I lived in my studio, I ate, breathed, and slept *Elfquest!* I was working against horrendous deadlines because not only was I working on finishing the series by a specific time, but we specifically had to have it out to premiere at the World Science Fiction Convention in Anaheim, California that year. We were having a big premiere party there. I was also working with my assistants on getting the fourth color volume colored. I was literally working around the clock. My health was failing. I was so involved with the characters and what was happening to them, because that's a very violent part of the story where we lose some favorite characters and so forth that, emotionally, I was pretty much of a wreck. I really was not thinking logically, and I don't know if I couldn't have done things in better proportion. That's how it happened. It's an experience I never want to go through again, and I think I can do work equally good without killing myself for it. But I think that happens when you're involved with too many things at once. Sometimes you can forget about yourself, and let yourself be consumed, and your project sort of takes over.

WEBER: *If you, say tomorrow, had to hand over* Elfquest *to people in the industry, are there people you would like to see do* Elfquest?

WENDY: Not right now.

RICHARD: Well, the answer to the question is basically no. But we have had the opportunity, from time to time, to work with some people who have demonstrated a sensitivity to *Elfquest* that we have found pleasant or refreshing. I don't think that we would be comfortable entrusting the entire thing to them, say, "Here it is, go, run with it", without being able to look over shoulders or check in from time to time.

WENDY: I've had particular trouble finding people who can draw the characters. I can find people who can draw bits of them. For instance, there are a number of women artists that I know that can do the facial expressions rather well. But their figure drawing is weak. They don't have the sense of chunkiness and mass that the characters need. There are some male artists that I know, and one of them has been my assistant, Joe Barruso, who had a very good feeling for animation and the chunkiness and mass of the characters. But the facial expressions weren't very subtle. To find an artist that has that combination, so far I haven't been able to come across one. There's either a weakness in one area or the other.

WEBER: Siege at Blue Mountain - *when it is coming?*

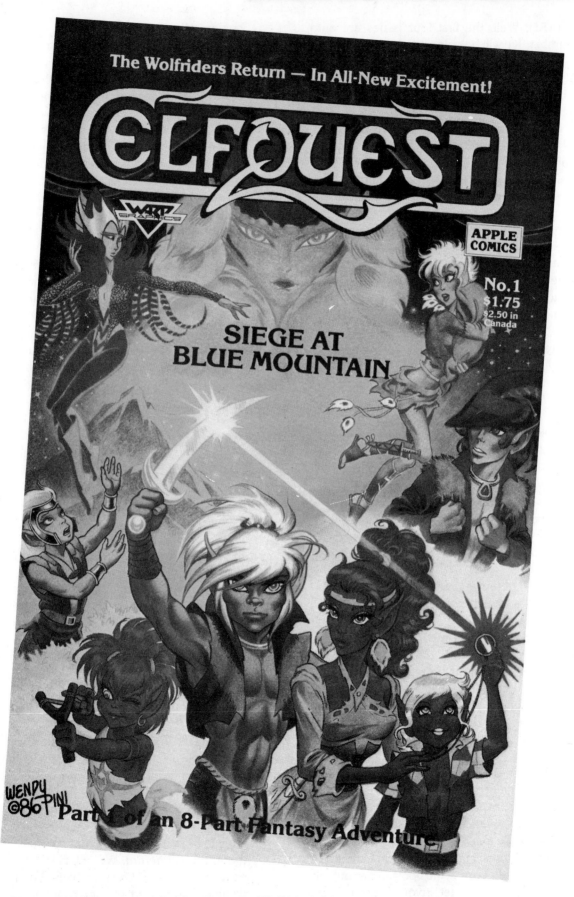

Elfquest: Siege at Blue Mountain — looking in on the Wolfriders three years after the first Quest ended.

RICHARD: Well, the first four issues are out. Issue number five will be going into production real soon now.

WENDY: Within the next month, I would guess. It's at the inker's right now.

RICHARD: All of it?

WENDY: All except four pages. Those are mine.

RICHARD: It should be out within a month. There are a lot of extenuating circumstances that have befallen the schedule of *Siege*, and where we used to agonize terribly over scheduling during the last series, for a lot of reasons, we're not agonizing over it this time. As Wendy said, there are ways to kill yourself, and there are ways not to kill yourself. And we really don't choose to kill ourselves, which is not to say that we deliberately want to go and be irresponsible. But, especially with the state of the market, not all of the reason for *Elfquest*'s slowness is up in Poughkeepsie. For example, if we don't get paid by the distributor for the previous issue, then we're not motivated terribly to get the next issue out on time to that distributor so he can fail to pay us again. Meanwhile, the printer wants to be paid for both. So there's this debilitating give-and-take.

WENDY: It's a tough time to be doing a series right now. It's a tough time to be emotionally involved with your baby right now. There are a number of independent companies now who are putting out a great quantity of product. And we watch various series die after four or five issues, and hear "Oh well, that's all right, we'll go into another one," and I suppose that's one way just to keep yourself out there on the stands. But it's kind of a throwaway way to look at the material you're producing.

RICHARD: It's also another reason why the only comic series coming from us is *Elfquest*. Now, we're also doing books, because we're in the process of publishing trade books, and a book is a one-shot project. Even if it's a series of books, though, you don't have the pressing monthly or bimonthly deadline. It's scheduled, and the book comes out on this date, and then you get involved in another really different project. There's a certain ease to be had from working that way as opposed to a continu-ous, grinding deadline.

WENDY: I've been talking to a number of people in the industry who are beginning to feel the burden of, say, having been ten or twelve years in that grind, and wondering, "Is this all there is?" We have discovered that you can go just so far in the comics field. And there comes a point where you can't really take your format any further. *Elfquest* has done everything it's possible to do with a comic book. We started out as an innovative, independent series, black and white, self published. We gained a huge readership — by the time we finished the twenty issue series, we were up to a circulation of 100,000. We were the first independent series to be licensed and reprinted by a mainstream comic company, Marvel Comics. We were the first graphic novel series produced in America to be marketed through Waldenbooks and B. Dalton's. There isn't any farther that *Elfquest* can go. All we can do is repeat ourselves. That's not what we want to do. In fact, my plans for the future, as far as working on *Elfquest*, are that I don't intend to do a series in black and white, in chapters, and have it come out five months later or whatever any more. The next *Elfquest* story that I do will be a nice, big, fat graphic novel, complete in its entirety, before anyone sees it. And I'm going to enjoy that much better! However long it takes to produce, I don't have to worry —

WEBER: *It'll be ready when it's ready!*

WENDY: Exactly. And it'll be very well-loved by me, and I'm looking forward to having the luxury of doing the work that way.

WEBER: *Can you give a little preview of what's to come?*

WENDY: You mean not just *Elfquest* projects, what else we've got going? Well, one thing I'm very excited about right now is *Law and Chaos*, which will be out in late November, early December.

RICHARD: Second half of November. This is a Father Tree Press book. I mentioned doing books earlier. In fact you've got one of our books right there, the *Gatherum*. We published that. Our first book was called *Chroma*, which was an art book dealing with the art of Alex Schomburg, who's a science fiction/comics illustrator. Well, in November, we will be doing *Law and Chaos*, which is

> "We have discovered that you can go just so far in the comics field...there comes a point where you can't take your format any further. *Elfquest* has done everything it's possible to do with a comic book."

another art book — and it's the account of Wendy's involvement with a project to single-handedly (laughter) animate the Michael Moorcock novel *Stormbringer*, which is about his character Elric — I guess Elric is really the first sword-and-sorcery anti-hero —

WENDY: He was the antithesis of Conan the Barbarian. Moorcock's intention was to do a character that was the complete opposite of Conan.

RICHARD: Anyway, Elric is an archetype. Wendy was involved with the character, a very moody, philosophical character.

WENDY: I read the book when I was sixteen years old and, even before I had met Richard, I had written to Moorcock and asked his permission to adapt it as a film project. I worked on it for about five years.

RICHARD: We've been talking here about the difficulties of doing animated films, seven million dollars, and she wanted to do one by herself (laughter)!

WENDY: Nobody told me I couldn't (laughter)!

RICHARD: Well, anyway, it turned out to be impossible to do for a number of reasons, which are gone into in the book. Wendy has provided the text. There are some hundreds of illustrations that she did that were never used, but that have survived to this day.

WENDY: Full color, every page.

RICHARD: We pulled out about 120-130 of the best of these, and the book has these illustrations plus Wendy's text. It's going to the printer next week, and we're very excited about this book.

People have been looking forward to it for a long time.

WENDY: It's the most personally revealing thing I have done because, in the text, I talk about — well, just as I spoke to you about the difficulties of getting the *Elfquest* series done, *Elfquest* was nowhere near, has never been, the kind of obsession with me that *Stormbringer* was when I was a teenager. I had literally dedicated my life to this project (laughter), this was my mystical ovation to Brahma or whatever (laughter). You know, that was way back in the flower child era, and my mind was expanded, and I just thought this was great. And so, everything that I did was built around getting this film done. And I talk a lot about obsession and what that has to do with creativity and what kind of energies you channel, and what you lose when you get into the grip of an obsession. I've never talked about this in public.

RICHARD: So that's November. Next year is *Elfquest's* tenth anniversary. The first issue of *Fantasy Quarterly* appeared in February of 1978, so 1988 is our ten year bash, blowout, kickoff, whatever. And we've got a lot of things planned. Volume Two of the *Gatherum* will come out in 1988, around springtime. We are planning to do all future *Elfquest* color volumes ourselves. We are planning to revamp the existing *Elfquest* color volumes and publish them ourselves. So '88 looks like a very busy, very exciting year.

WENDY: And who knows, by then the film might be in production (laughter).

WEBER: *Which film, the* Elfquest *one, or —*

WENDY: The *Elfquest* one (laughter).

Another look into *Law and Chaos*.

Stormbringer, I think someone else will do (laughter). I fantasize that someone will pick up *Law and Chaos* and flip through it, and say, "Why, here are our model charts, let's go," you know, just make the film (laughter).

RICHARD: In which case I say, "Let's talk" (laughter).

WENDY: I think they'd better talk to Michael Moorcock first.

WEBER: *Then there'll be* Law and Chaos II, *based on...*

RICHARD: If they use your models, they talk to us.

WEBER: *I should have been a lawyer.*

WENDY: It's fascinating, isn't it?

RICHARD: Lawyers are the only ones who win anything anyway.

WEBER: *What comics do you guys read, when you have time? Any that you follow?*

RICHARD: I guess I speak for myself here — I don't follow anything. We both used to be fans in the mid and late 1960s. That was a wonderful time to be a comics fan because, particularly, Marvel was just beginning to feel its oats, and it was the new kid on the block, and it had the fresh Stan Lee-Jack Kirby-Steve Ditko feel to everything. In the early 70s everything seemed to stagnate, and there have been ups and downs, and ups and downs, and now comics, at least as far as I'm concerned, have gotten so commercial.

WENDY: Cynical.

RICHARD: Cynical. There's such a pressure to have blockbuster hits, to create knockoffs of what the other guy's blockbuster hit is, that the good stuff is few and far between. I think that, again, for myself, I got caught up in Frank Miller's *Daredevil*, I got caught up for a while in Walt Simonson's *Thor*. I enjoyed Frank Miller's *Dark Knight*. I can say I enjoyed it without saying I agreed with it. I think I can do that. I'm kind of following to see what John Byrne does with *Superman*.

WENDY: We tend to follow what our friends in the industry do. We tend to keep up and see what they're doing. Personally, I'm thrilled right now that First Comics and Eclipse Comics are bringing out *Lone Wolf and Cub* and the *Kamui* series because, particularly the *Kamui* series, the artwork of Sanpei Shirato, was a very strong influence on the look of *Elfquest*. And *Siege at Blue Mountain* in particular is my tribute to the look of the drawing in the *Kamui* series.

RICHARD: Wendy was plowing through that series in the original Japanese *years* before Japanimation became popular in this country.

WENDY: After I'd moved back east and married Richard, I think it was in '74 or '75, we met a guy who had been living in Japan for some time. I think it was a military connection. He had a large collection of Japanese comics. Among the things he had for sale was this enormous volume, with a beautiful red cover, of the *Kamui* comics. And that was the first look I had at it. Bought it right on the spot. Didn't know what the story was about, but the tremendous cinematic storytelling! So the fact is that *Kamui* and *Lone Wolf and Cub* are available now for readers to get a really good taste of Japanese storytelling — *for the Japanese* — you see, a lot of readers are exposed now to Japanese comics and animation and moviemaking that is aimed at a Western audience. And, as such, that sort of stuff is very self-conscious and not really true to the Japanese mentality or to their own basic, historical way of telling the stories. *Lone Wolf and Cub* and *Kamui* are integral to the Japanese philosophy of life. Very *bushido* (laughter). The translations seem to be extremely faithful, very simple, very beautiful, very tasteful, and I just think it's wonderful that these books are available in this country, and so true to the Japanese philosophy.

WEBER: *And they're being accepted in the Western world.*

The Japanese influence...

WENDY: They seem to be. I have no idea what the sales are, but I'm hoping.

RICHARD: Sales are probably good. The only possible fly in the ointment is that the fans of Japanimation are picking these up and seeing, only superficially, that they are a Ninja story, or a Samurai story. And they're not seeing the thousand of years of culture that are behind this way of storytelling, and these stories. If they miss that, then they might as well not buy it and they might as well look at *Star Blazers* again.

WENDY: To truly appreciate Japanese comics, there is so much for us to learn from their style of storytelling. You have to understand what a hand gesture means because they're different for men and women. It's almost like *Kabuki*, like watching a *Kabuki* play. Once you've learned that subtle second language to the artwork, it makes it all the more fascinating.

WEBER: *We were talking about the independents and the commercialism of comics and you're familiar with the* Jon Sable *soon-to-be TV series, and I understand that they're taking the comic, ending the run, and retitling it, just calling it* Sable *(like the TV series will be) and starting with #1. That sort of bothers me that they would do that. I under-*

...from the early adventures of Kamui. © 1988 Viz.

stand the reasoning behind it...

RICHARD: Rick Obadiah is a businessman, and a good one. I've sat down and shared conversation with him. He's very savvy. I'd be willing to bet that the decisions he has made, is making, will make, are good for some aspect of the commercialization of the *Sable* property. Aesthetically, I don't know. I have different feelings about that. I might say, "He's going with what somebody behind a desk at a network headquarters is requesting that he do." Is he selling out? I don't know. I mean there are those who would say he is, there are those who would shrug their shoulders and say, "Who cares?"

WENDY: In the long run, it all depends on what it looks like when it gets on screen. Will Eisner made no secret of the fact that he detested *The Spirit* special (laughter).

RICHARD: What we hope is that we do not get to that point. When we were dealing with CBS, they made a lot of requests of us to change the concepts and feeling of *Elfquest*. Some of those requests, with the help of some good writers, we were able to accommodate. And we felt what we came up with was true. Some of the later requests, where they wanted us to go further and further and further away from what we had originally created, we finally had to throw up our hands and say "We can't do this!"

WENDY: No, we couldn't countenance that.

RICHARD: We just can't stomach it, really. And so we didn't. That's one of the reasons why we're not on CBS Saturday morning. There's artistic rigidity, there's artistic flexibility, and then there's selling out. I think the two extremes are not good. But I think that middle ground — there's a way to stay integral to what you have, and yet work with other people to achieve an agreed-upon goal.

WENDY: The term "selling out" is a very subjective thing. We were accused of selling out simply by having Marvel reprint *Elfquest* (laughter). In some areas, some fans were very disturbed that we didn't remain "pure".

RICHARD: That's because those fans hate Marvel.

WEBER: *And also, those fans want to be kind of cultish — it's THEIRS, it's THEIR book.*

WENDY: It belongs to them.

RICHARD: And I can understand that because, back when we were reading Marvel, when it was, as I said, the new kid, the number two, "we try harder", we felt a certain betrayal, whether or not we were entitled to feel that, by Marvel's viewpoint. We felt it when they got successful, and they started wearing their success. Now there are fans who feel about *Elfquest*, you know, "we discovered it", "you and us against the world"; but the fact that they feel that would never stop us from attempting to get *Elfquest* to a wider audience, which is why we signed the deal with Marvel.

WEBER: *One more item about commercialization and we'll go on to a couple of other areas. Have either of you seen the new* Batman: Son of the Demon *graphic novel that just came out?*

RICHARD: Yeah.

WENDY: I haven't seen it yet.

WEBER: *There's a scene in there, and maybe it's because I grew up on DC — I picked up Marvels, too, but it was mainly DC — a scene where Batman literally disrobes and goes to bed with Talia. I don't have any rational explanation for it, but it really disturbed me, even though I'm an adult and —*

WENDY: That's probably the little boy in you that grew up with Batman.

WEBER: *To do that with a character —*

WENDY: I don't see anything wrong with it (laughter).

WEBER: *I really don't either, but I can't separate the discomfort I felt —*

RICHARD: Possibly, the source of that feeling is that, for years and years and years and years, Batman has been a shadowy figure, mysterious. I mean he's gone through periods of being very camp and very silly, but if you go back to the origins, the idea of the Batman is a terrifying, dark figure of night. And perhaps somewhere in that mind that we all had when we started reading comics, we think that there are some things that we are not meant to know. You don't see Captain America sitting on a toilet!

WENDY: Well, I think it's also the nature of the superhero himself. If you stop to think about it, even the costume of a superhero is a closed unit. I think the Silver Surfer is the ultimate expression of that. He cannot have sex because he's coated with silver (laughter). But the skin-tight costume is a very enclosing kind of thing. It's constricting. And you don't tend to think of the character as being flesh and blood. You think of the costume as being the character.

RICHARD: There's not a man in there. There's a foreskin there. And you know that Bruce Wayne

wears a three-piece suit, and you see him walking around talking to Commissioner Gordon. But with the Batman — it's not quite Bruce Wayne in there, there's an elemental kind of force which, again, going back to *Dark Knight*, that's, I think, one of the main things Frank Miller was examining. This mythological force that transcends flesh-and-bloodedness. And that may be the source of that discomfort.

WENDY: We've often gotten letters, and even with *Siege at Blue Mountain*, we get letters from people who are disturbed when we show nudity or eroticism of any kind with the characters. "I can do without it" they say, "it's okay for you to show everything else, but I can really do without all that mushy stuff." And let's face it, our society is still repressed when it comes to sexuality. We have no problem with showing blood and violence. I was just going to say about the Batman character that Batman has BLED for us (laughter) over the years many, many times, and in situations that could be considered subliminally erotic. Maggie Thompson and I got off on a kick, an interview that we did once that touched on the subject of how women respond to violence and how underneath it all —

RICHARD: Suffering.

WENDY: — and suffering, as an erotic stimulus. So the Batman has done that for us, in spades, over the years. So what is really disturbing about his actual sexuality being depicted?

WEBER: *The answer is, there really isn't anything. And I wouldn't write and say, "Take it out," or I wouldn't skip that page.*

WENDY: Yeah, but you had that little twinge (laughter).

WEBER: *I did, and I couldn't believe I was seeing it, and I went back and checked again, and you're right, that is okay, but —*

RICHARD: We grew up and we have these impressions imbedded. I have no idea what impressions are being imbedded in the minds and creative souls of kids who are starting to read comics now, because we started back then, and you started at a certain time. You never let them go. They're always there. So if the Batman was dark and spooky and not quite human, to see him as ultimately human

> "...the costume of a superhero is a closed unit...the skin-tight costume is a very enclosing kind of thing. It's constricting. And you don't tend to think of the character as flesh and blood. You think of the costume as being the character."

From *Siege at Blue Mountain*: Violence is all right, but eroticism is a no-no?

might be bothersome. We're friends with John Byrne. We go and eat dinner at his house, and he comes and eats dinner at our house, and I think he's a wonderful talent. But I don't know if I'll ever quite accept his *Superman* the way I fondly remember *Superman* from the late 1960s. The Weisinger stories, which are absolutely absurd and silly, but nonetheless, they represent an essence of Superman that is very important to me.

WENDY: You don't even analyze why it's important. I mean, ultimately, if you try to analyze why it's important to you, those wonderful childish love affairs, they fall apart (laughter).

RICHARD: (in a big voice) Ah may not know comics, but Ah know what Ah like (laughter).

WEBER: *Let's talk about, quickly, children's entertainment. What is good on TV, what's bad, what's being done right?*

RICHARD: What's good on TV is a statue that I brought home from a flea market. It sits right on top, and it's very pretty. That's what's good on TV.

WENDY: What he means is, he bought a nude lady with a clock in her stomach, or the equivalent (laughter). What's good on TV is anything that has to do with real human experience. One of the things that I wanted to say on the radio interview earlier that I didn't get a chance to was that we don't believe children should be protected from anything. We think that everything, in proportion and in perspective, is appropriate in children's storytelling, even unto violence and eroticism.

WEBER: *When you say this, do you mean children's storytelling, or...*

WENDY: Well, storytelling for all ages, actually, but storytelling that is accessible to children. *Elfquest* is not aimed at any particular age group. Our audience tends to be in the high school/adult age group.

RICHARD: But it is accessible to everyone.

WENDY: It's accessible to children, and they interpret it on their level. We don't feel that any element of life is inappropriate in the telling of a good yarn. Whether it's dealing with questions of morals, responsibility to society —

RICHARD: Love, life, death.

WENDY: — love, life, death, all of those things that are universal experiences are appropriate for children to handle, and they can handle it, provided that it's done in proportion, with perspective, with guidance. We give our younger readers some difficult things to deal with sometimes. For instance, one of the major themes in *Siege at Blue Mountain* right now, in a very subtle way, is child abuse. And it's done in such a way that different age groups can perceive what we're saying about child abuse at different levels. And what we are hoping is that this sparks discussion among people who trust each other, whether it's parents and children, friends and friends, teenagers among themselves, whatever. We don't feel that children should be protected from controversy, we don't feel that children should be protected from thinking. And any storytelling that

Two-Edge: Child abuse on the World of Two Moons.

prevents you from thinking is not good storytelling.

RICHARD: Unfortunately, that's most of what's on television, whether it's prime time, Saturday morning, weekday afternoon, or you name it.

WENDY: The toy companies don't want you to think. They want you to buy. So Filmation does *Marshal Bravestarr* or Rankin/Bass does *Thundercats*. And they do stories with heavy-handed morals as a sop to the parents. And after the story's done, the characters come out and tell you what the moral was, even though the child, at age two, is smart enough to get what the moral message was. It's all a sop to the parents so that they will say, "Oh, that's good stuff, I'll go out and buy the toy. It's okay." Antithink.

WEBER: *Is there anything on TV you would let children watch? You don't have any children.*

RICHARD: We do not have children, and again, for myself, I watch very little television. So I couldn't tell you. Honestly, I'd like to be in the position of helping to get *Elfquest* on, and I could point to that and say, "Yeah, I think that's good" (laughter). I'm only being half-egotistical here. There are shows, I guess, that are highly praised by people, perhaps *The Cosby Show*, which deals with a family situation. Or *Family Ties*, which deals with, from time to time, issues that face kids. I guess perhaps I'm cynical, though, in that I think if a child — and that can be anywhere from three through eighteen — receives a half-hour dose of something that could be considered good once a week, that's not enough. It doesn't stick. It doesn't last. Unless it simply reinforces what's already in that person's life. There's a family structure, or some kind of support structure - that reinforces.

WENDY: And the kids, as inarticulate as they sometimes are, are telling the producers and creators, just as they've been telling us all these years that we've been doing with *Elfquest* exactly what they want. I think more interaction of parents with children, more conversation, will make kids more trusting and more able to say what they want without worrying about getting slapped in the mouth. But kids write to us, they write to other comics creators, and tell people what they like. They like the feeling of family and belonging. They like the feeling of a value system. They like the feeling of a direction. They like the feeling that a character might grow and learn after making a mistake, and that there isn't a punishment for all time. They really do relate to that. That's what they want.

WEBER: *Here's a scary thought. Is that, the value system and the feeling of family, is fantasy the only place the kids can get that?*

WENDY: Sometimes. That's why they become fantasy junkies. You go to a convention, you know who they are, the "moonshots", the ones that drift around with that look in their eyes. You can spot them a mile away. They are the ones who live through fantasy because life is simply too unbearable for them. They get addicted to it. It's like a drug. And I really feel bad when creators put down fans and talk about them as, you know, lump them all together into that moonshot class. I feel very strongly for these lost ones, as irritating as they can be, as much as they can get on your nerves, I feel very sorry that this is their only source of feeling that they belong to something, that they live in fandom because they don't have family at home, or an ability to talk to friends, or whatever.

WEBER: *It becomes their family.*

WENDY: It becomes their family. The *Star Trek* junkies, the *Doctor Who* junkies, the *Elfquest* junkies, they're all out there. And they are all sucking off something that's giving them a sense of purpose. I don't think this is healthy. I don't think this is right, and I speak from experience because I went that route with Elric when I was a kid. I wouldn't encourage any kid to become an *Elfquest* junkie, or any other kind of junkie. Proportion is what we're talking about. We were just talking about that earlier. Proportion in all ways, in storytelling; any story that has an ax to grind is going to burn itself out eventually, like the nihilistic comics that Richard was talking about earlier. Any ax to grind eventually has its limits. Human experience doesn't.

WEBER: *I also wanted to ask you about the labeling/rating controversy. I think I have an idea where you stand.*

RICHARD: Well, I think the whole flap that happened when DC announced its rating system has been done to death. Basically, my feeling on that is, I'm in agreement with the people who walked out, who said that they walked out not because there was a rating system being considered, but because it had been considered and imposed without any input from them. In other words, their work was going to have this thing done to it without any input from them. That was wrong. I think ratings are a silly idea because I don't see how the heck they can be consistent. I have a difficult time envisioning a title like *Spider-Man* having a consistent rating. To borrow the movie ratings, let's say *Spider-Man* is assigned a PG-13. That means that every story must fall within the bounds of a PG-13 comic book story. That means you can't have a gentle, "G" rated *Spider-Man* story, and you can't have something grittier that would gain it an "R". You can't do it with a series. I have absolutely no problem with advisories. We used advisories once on *Elfquest*. An advisory is just a little note that says this contains such-and-so and such-and-so. This contains violence, this contains some scenes of nudity, this contains adult themes, however you want to word it, some bit of communication from publisher to consumer. That doesn't bother me in the least. Ratings — I don't think it's ever gonna happen in the comics. You see books now that say "for mature readers", but that's an advisory. That's not a rating. The ratings thing is mostly hot air, and it's going to dissipate before we're really aware it was an issue. You watch.

One of the scenes that carried an advisory notice: War is ugly and brutal, and don't imagine otherwise.

From the sketchbook — studies of Cutter, Blood of Ten Chiefs.

Games People Play

It was, perhaps, inevitable. The world of Elfquest is so well realized, and its denizens so well fleshed out that it was only a matter of time before readers began to dream up their own adventures. Sometimes they would use the characters that Wendy and Richard had already created; sometimes they would imagine their own elves and trolls, tribes and lands. By this time the phenomonon of role-playing games, usually exemplified by Dungeons and Dragons, was in full flower, and fans began to ask when an Elfquest game might show up. Since neither Wendy nor Richard are gamers, it became necessary for them to find people who had the ability and experience to take a world teeming with established characters and environments and to boil them down into their component attributes. (What *is* Cutter's strength, numerically, compared to Picknose's, anyway?) Luckily the Pinis found not one but two gaming companies that were more than equal to the challenge. One, Chaosium (P.O. Box 6302, Albany, California 94706), turned Elfquest into a role-playing game; the other, Mayfair Games (P.O. Box 48539, Niles, Illinois 60648), developed a board game. On the following pages is reproduced some of the artwork that Wendy has done for "what-if" tribes of elves that inhabit the World of Two moons — if only in the imaginations of the players.

HE'D LEAVE THE BRAT HANGING ON A *BRANCH* SOMEWHERE AND END UP IN A *GAME* DOWN IN THE *TROLL CAVERNS,* CHEATING OLD KING *GREYMUNG'S* GUARDS OUT OF *BELTS, BUCKLES, BRITCHES AND ALL!*

This page and the next two: scenes of plains dwellers and sea elves.

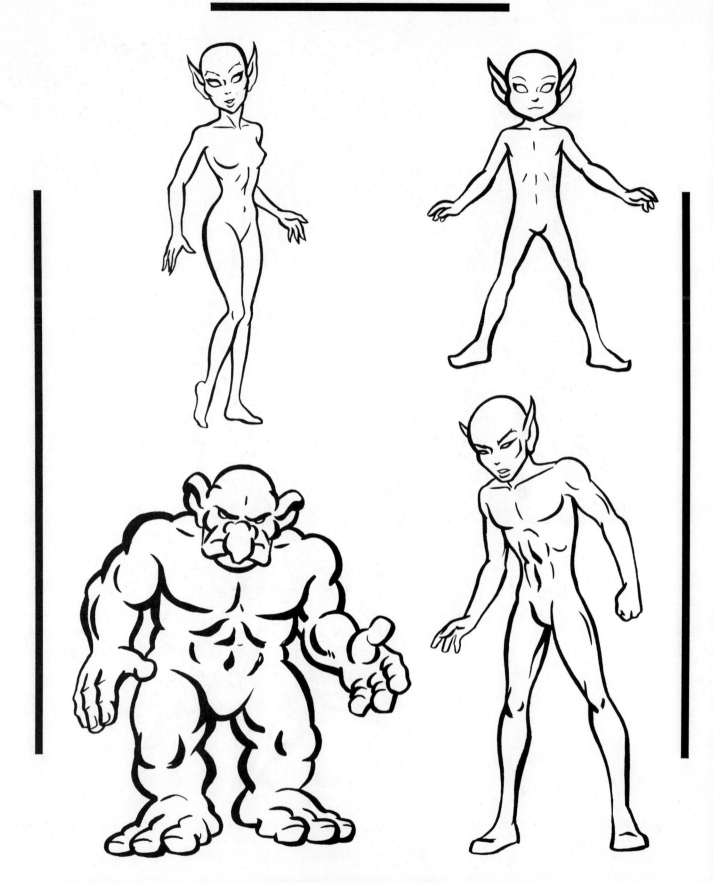

Mannequin drawings of elf body types; the player will add hair, costume, and any other features to complete the character he or she has created for the game.

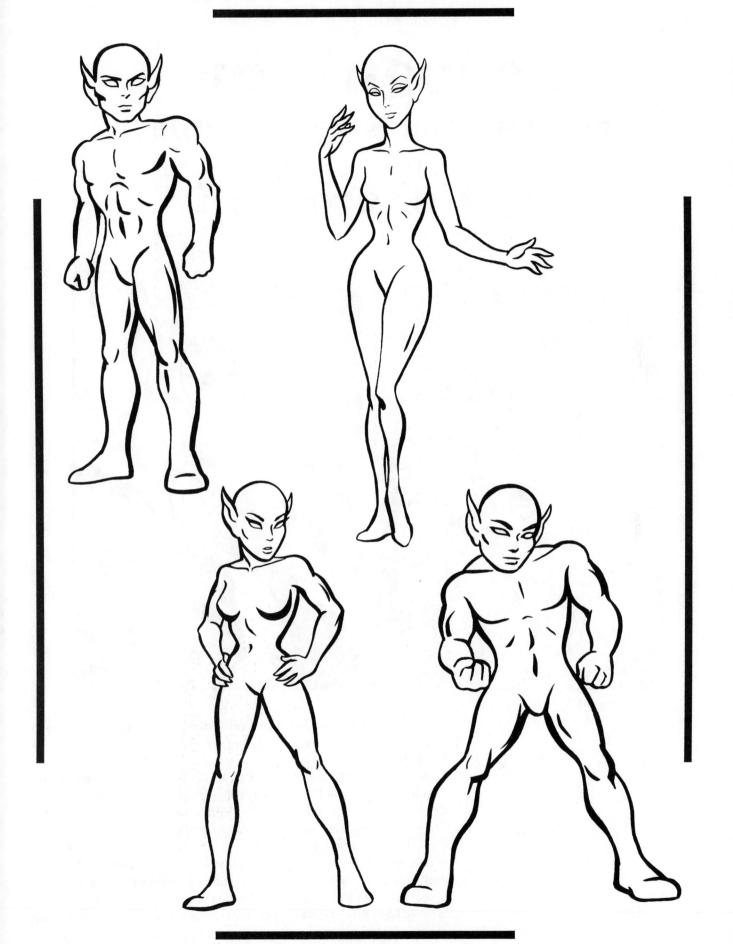

Recognition
(or: How Loud Is <u>Your</u> Reptile?)
by Richard Pini

Recognition strikes!

One of the more commented upon of the phenomena that have been introduced into the stewpot of fantasy through *Elfquest* is that of **Recognition**.

At first it seemed that Recognition was little more than a particularly elfin form of "love at first sight" (or what Mario Puzo referred to in *The Godfather* as "the thunderbolt"). And, admittedly, when it happened to Cutter and Leetah in *Elfquest* #2 (*all issue numbers refer to the original WaRP Graphics editions of the series - Ed.*) there was not much else given in that issue to explain that Recognition was anything more. The word itself is not used until *EQ#3*, as Treestump attempts to explain what is wrong with his chief, and only a cryptic thought by the Suntoucher late in *EQ#2* hints that what has happened between Wolfrider and Sun Village maid might be something of some import.

Then, as events progress, through "The Challenge" (*EQ*#3) and "Wolfsong" (*EQ*#4) to the resolution in "Voice of the Sun" (*EQ*#5) — and beyond, into issue #6, "The Quest Begins" — various bits of Recognition lore come to light. Recognition, it seems, creates in the pair of afflicted elves a strong urge to mate with each other; the imperative is so powerful that to deny it is to court sickness and perhaps even death. Also, Recognition ensures that the mating will result in offspring (elf children are quite rare otherwise) and further, that those children will express the best genetic qualities of both parents. In later issues (the sequence in *Blue Mountain*) it comes out that Recognized couples need not stay with each other as long as the sexual and generative imperatives are attended to. Dewshine and Tyldak just do not like each other, but they are able to reconcile their differences sufficiently to meet Recognition's demands. Thus freed, Dewshine continues in her relationship with Scouter.

AND...

WE... *CAN'T* BE LIFEMATES.

I KNOW...

AS HE SEES HER--

--SO SHE SEES HIM.

BUT WE *CAN* SET EACH OTHER FREE.

Dewshine and Tyldak meet halfway, as each sees the shape of the other's inner being.

Since the end of the series with *Elfquest* #20, other facets of Recognition have been thought out and examined, and some conclusions have been drawn. A couple that has Recognized does not necessarily stay together for life; lifemating is a decision of choice, whereas Recognition is imposed. this is not to say that Recognized couples can't lifemate — Cutter and Leetah seem to be well into that category — but it is not necessary. Given that, it is also possible that the partners in Recognition may, after a suitable period of time (something normally on the order of scores to hundreds of years) may experience Recognition again with different partners. It is possible that one of the partners may die, either before or after the act of procreation. If the partner dies after, the surviving elf can Recognize again, and there will be no (or few) ill effects following the loss of the partner — at least from the point of view of Recognition. If one of the elves dies before the Recognition is consummated, the survivor will not die, but will experience that "sickness" that comes from the unfulfilled urge. However, he or she will recover, as it is not the function of Recognition to kill elves.

All of which is well and good. Recognition, then, seems to be at its basic level a genetic "device" to produce high quality elf children. It is selective and irresistible. It always works. But *why* is it?

The answer lies in two qualities possessed by the original "High Ones" (which, to avoid terminological confusion with the elfin "High Ones" who came out of the castle in *EQ#1*, shall henceforth be called "the Coneheads," for obvious reasons) even before they left their homeworld to explore the cosmos. These beings were both essentially immortal (meaning that they lived at least a very long time; for all practical purposes, anything over ten thousand years equals infinity), and they were telepathic. With immortality came great reductions in the urges, both physical and social, to bear young. (Which is not to say the folks were ascetic; they had the opportunity to do away totally with physical form and yet chose to remain "clothed in matter" because, simply, it felt good. They still enjoyed sensation, but sex itself and its attendant pleasures seem to have fallen into disuse.) With telepathy came the ability to know another mind on as deep a level as the sender and receiver desired.

The Coneheads make the choice that will define their nature for all time.

WE, FOR I EXISTED BY THEN, LEARNED TO SEND OUR SPIRITS "OUT." THESE LITTLE DEATHS TEMPTED US TO ABANDON OUR BODIES ALTOGETHER, FOR IT IS VERY PEACEFUL WITHOUT FLESH AND THE SENSES.

BUT WE CHOSE *FORM* AND ALL THE PLEASURES AND PAINS THAT GO WITH IT! WE CHOSE AN IMMORTALITY SEASONED WITH *CHANCE* RATHER THAN TRANQUILITY.

THERE WAS NO NEW GROWTH OR KNOWLEDGE TO BE HAD ON OUR FINISHED WORLD, SO ONCE AGAIN WE LOOKED TO THE STARS...AND TO A NEW GOAL-- --EXPERIENCE!

The Coneheads were also shapechangers, which is to say that over long evolutionary time their psychokinetic powers of matter manipulation became so finely tuned that they could shape the very stuff of which they were made. this power operated down to the genetic level; if a Conehead changed into a toad, he or she could mate with toads and produce offspring (the partner would have to be a very big toad, however, as mass is conserved). The mind of the shifter would retain its Coneheadedness, although the longer the change was in effect, the blurrier the memories and thoughts of the thinker would become. After a while the Conehead-toad would think and respond to stimuli very much like a real toad, and likely would forget how to change back. (The severity of this problem is in direct proportion to the psychological difference between Conehead and imitated being; i.e., it's more dangerous for a brunette Conehead to change into a gnat than into a blonde Conehead.)

Take all this, put into a pot and stir. The Coneheads went into space to explore the myriad worlds to be found. One group chanced upon the World of Two Moons during its so-called middle ages, when elfin mythology was rife. The Coneheads, desirous of learning about the human culture they observed, shapeshifted into elf form, the better to learn from the (ostensibly) superstitious natives. They *were* elves at that point, as their "magic" would have altered their genetic material elfwards.

Then the trolls rebelled, the castle-ship (which the Coneheads had also reformed to resemble the structures they saw on the world below) crashed, and the (now) High Ones found that, for whatever reason, they could not muster the power to shift back (or indeed to do much of anything they were used to doing - note *EQ#1* and #20). The High Ones were stuck. And the need for something that would turn into Recognition began.

One theory concerning the structure of the human brain is that it consists of three "layers," arranged like the layers of a wrinkly onion. The deeper one probes into a brain, the older or more primitive one finds the feelings and functions of that portion of tissue. The innermost layer is the limbic or so-called "reptile" part of the brain, responsible for basic territorial and reproductive urges; the middle layer is the "mammal" brain, which gives rise to the urge to take care of young, and the outermost, most recent layer is the "human" brain or cortex, wherein higher cerebration and the writing of articles takes place.

It is thought that, even though *homo sapiens* on Earth represents to date the pinnacle of cognitive evolution, he still functions in large part according to the dictates of those earlier brains he carries within his skull. In particular, overlaid with motherhood and conscience though it may be, down in the bottom of the brain there is a drooling reptile who wants sex. Period. This may be simplistic, but it goes a long way toward explaining Recognition.

Even though they may have been vastly further along their evolutionary scale than man is along his, the Coneheads still started out in the same places — the primordial soup, the swamp, the reptile-infested jungle. No matter how subdued the early brain's impulses may have become by layer upon layer of high-level cortex, they must still have existed. Though the primitive reptile's shout of "Want sex! Want to reproduce!" was probably reduced to a mere whisper, subordinate to the massive conscious mentation of the rest of the brain, it was not silenced. It still spoke, though on a subconscious level.

And the Coneheads were telepathic.

When the castle-ship crash landed upon the World of Two Moons, the Coneheads were essentially trapped in the elfin form they had taken before the accident that stranded them. They were now the High Ones of Wolfrider memory-legend. they were scattered to the four corners of the compass by the primitive humans who attacked them (*EQ#1*) and were forced to attempt survival in a hostile environment. Even though they were still technically immortal (their shapeshifting would not have affected that) they soon discovered that there were plenty of ways in which the world could kill them. And deep down in the basements of their minds, the reptiles were remembering what the minds themselves had forgotten: that one kind of insurance against death is progeny.

So the reptiles started yelling for all they were worth, *"Hey, you up there, either you start getting it on or we're all going to die! You hear me?"* Now, had the High Ones not been telepathic, nothing more would have happened and there would have been no *Elfquest* because all the High Ones would have died thousands of years before Cutter was born. However, as mentioned in the EQ novelization *Journey to Sorrow's End* the High Ones managed to relearn, by watching animals and indigenous humans, what sex was all about. They began to experiment, goaded subconsciously by the reptile brains within them. *"Yeah! It feels **good**, doesn't it? You can do it - you **want** to! You know you do!"* And because the High Ones were telepathic, and because the reptiles could "pirate" a bit of that communication between individuals, the experimentation was hastened:

Reptile John: *"Hey! Anybody out there? I'm horny as hell and this yo-yo doesn't know the meaning of the word."*

Reptile Sue: *"Hello? I thought I just heard something...nice."*

Reptile John: *"Do you mean I'm not alone? Come to papa! I'll get this big lump to co-operate if it kills me! Hey, upstairs! You got the parts — now* **use** *them!"*

And two High Ones, who probably had not thought about sex in untold centuries, rediscover the joy inherent in trying to create little High Ones.

Natural selection takes a hand in the development of Recognition as well. It is easy to imagine that the reptile brains in certain of the original High Ones either had stronger "voices" than did others, or else were able to cast more of these voices onto the telepathic "carrier wave" generated by the High Ones' subconscious minds. whatever the method, those stronger reptiles were able to get their host bodies to participate more often in producing offspring, which thereby had the effect of concentrating the reptilian ability to shout *"I want sex!"* and be heard by a receptive mind (and where the mind goes, the body follows), which made the shouting louder and the receiving easier, and so on.

Eventually, things would have gotten to the point that the reptiles,

Leetah is playing hard to get, and Cutter feels the effects.

while still operating on a subconscious level (though loudly to each other), would be able to communicate more than just the desire for sex. They would have some kind of understanding of the genetic makeup of their hosts. (Remember, the conscious minds of the Coneheads could manipulate the matter of their own bodies down to the genetic level, so the potential for understanding this makeup must have permeated those minds.) At some point, an individual reptile would have started shouting, *"Hey out there! I'm horny! Not only that, but I'm good looking, with great eyes. Only trouble is, the ol' hearing's not so hot. Any available partners out there with fantastic hearing? We could make a heck of a kid, with good eyes* **and** *ears. How about it?"* And if there were a receptive reptile in the area whose host filled the bill, the two would start talking and pretty soon, bingo. It was the equivalent of the Personals column in the local swingers' newspaper. And it began creating elves with increased genetic potential.

From this point it is only a small step to Recognition as it is known in the *Elfquest* saga. As the reptile brains became more and more communicative, constantly shouting their genetic requests in to telepathic æther, competition and natural selection would continue to favor those who could make the best connections the fastest. Eventually, the reptiles would stop *asking* the hosts to participate, and would start *demanding*. (This may be taking anthropomorphism to the limit, but if it works, use it.) Reptile John XXIII might see in Reptile Sue XVIII some attractive genetic potential and yell to his host, *"Go get her or I'll make you so sick, I promise!"* The elfin maid's reptile is making similar unsubtle, non-negotiable demands of her landlady. Thus Recognition. From a certain point of view it is the natural result of increasingly successful sexual blackmail on the part of each reptile brain over its host. However, the overall effect has been to strengthen the elf race on the World of Two Moons to the point where it can be considered out of danger of extinction. And, in at least some cases, having a wonderful time doing so. Ask Skywise.

The exception that demonstrates the rule?
Kahvi and Rayek discuss the fine points.

From Elfland to Tinseltown (Part 2)

When we last left our intrepid heroes, the Wolfriders...

The comment was made in the introduction to Part One of this article, back in *Gatherum* Volume One, that if any characters were born natural for animation, the Wolfriders were those characters. To which can be added as well, if ever there was a story that was made for movement on the silver screen, it is *Elfquest*. *Gatherum* One was first published in 1981, just about the time when the idea of an *Elfquest* animated movie was starting to take off. It's been seven years since then, and what a roller-coaster ride it's been! Some of the events of those years are discussed in the two interviews elsewhere in this volume, but for those who want a condensed version, here goes. In 1981 the Canadian animation studio Nelvana approached Wendy and Richard with a proposal to produce an *Elfquest* animated film. They had the story for two years and ultimately decided they wanted to do a live-action film instead. The Pinis said no to that, and turned to a smaller animation studio in Pennsylvania. Things looked promising there until it became apparent that the studio wanted a much larger share of the pie than they originally indicated. Back to square one. Wendy and Richard began to investigate opening a studio right in Poughkeepsie where they live. It's still an attractive idea — the next $5 million that comes by that isn't doing anything, they'll no doubt start groundbreaking. Round about 1985-6 the CBS television network made interested noises, looking to develop *Elfquest* into a Saturday morning adventure cartoon series. It was a good idea at first. Then the network kept moving the potential show to earlier and earlier in the morning, which meant the stories had to be aimed at a younger and younger audience. Pretty soon *Elfquest* had become "Elf Babies" and neither CBS nor the Pinis were happy. So long CBS. However, in the development process, a lot of artwork was done — character charts, concept paintings, storyboards — and a selection has been reproduced here. In the meantime, Wendy and Richard are still plugging away at bringing the adventures of Cutter and company to a theatre near you.

What an animated *Elfquest* could look like. A production cel drawn by Wendy, inked and painted by Chelsea Animation of New York, with background by Johnnie Vita.

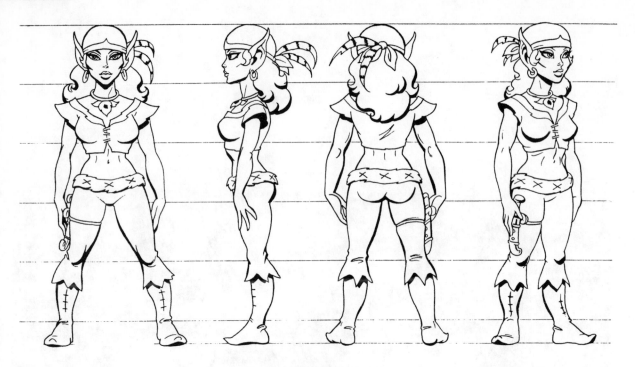

NIGHTFALL

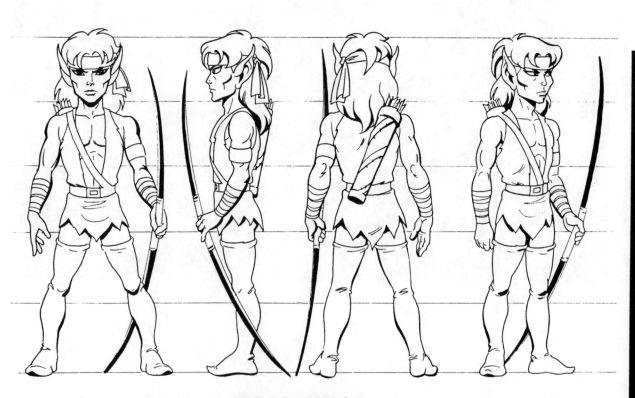

STRONGBOW

On this and the following two pages — model charts for several of the characters, giving bodily proportions for the animators to follow to achieve a consistent look.

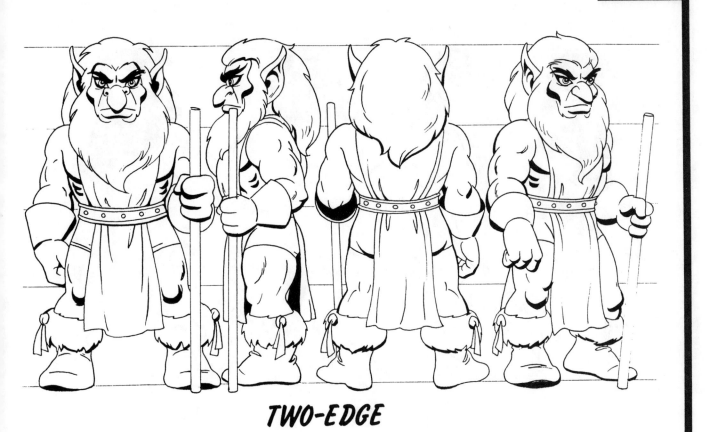

TWO-EDGE

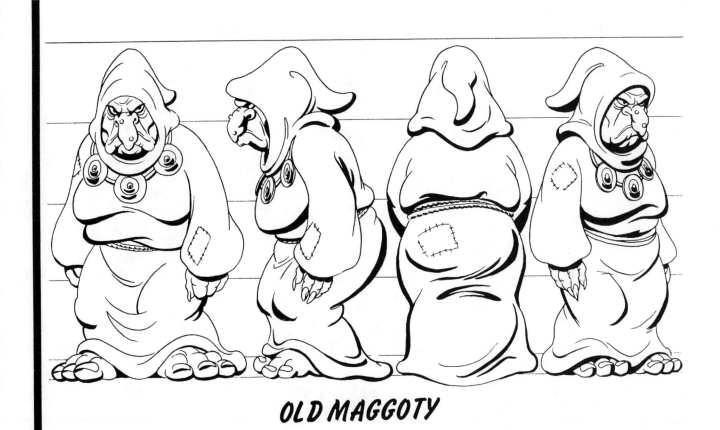

OLD MAGGOTY

PICKNOSE

TRINKET

Different views of Leetah's head and torso — again, a guide for the animators.

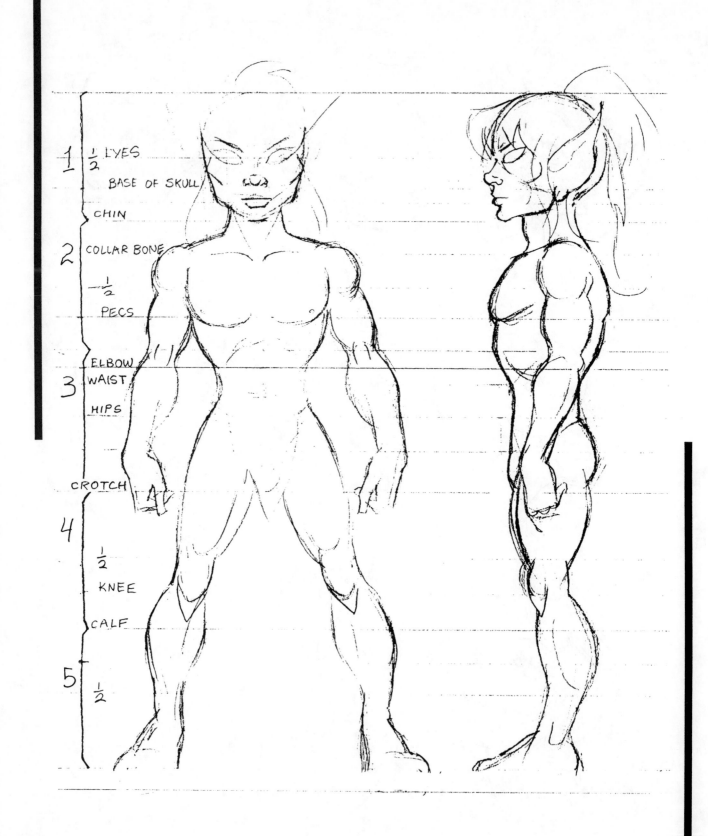

1 1/2 EYES
          BASE OF SKULL
       CHIN
2 COLLAR BONE
   —1/2
       PECS

   ELBOW
3 WAIST
   HIPS

CROTCH
4
   1/2
   KNEE
   CALF
5 1/2

More detailed model chart of Cutter, giving exact proportions, à la the anatomy books...

...and in costume.

" LITTLE TROLL LOST "

" DOMESTIC BLISS "

This and next page — several concept paintings illustrating episodes and events
from the proposed CBS Saturday morning television show.

"CHILDREN OF THE HIGH ONES"

"THE BLACK BEAR"

Sketchbook

Bits and pieces
from here and there

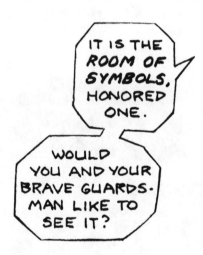

IT IS THE *ROOM OF SYMBOLS,* HONORED ONE.

WOULD YOU AND YOUR BRAVE GUARDSMAN LIKE TO SEE IT?

Concept drawings of Scouter and Dewshine for *Siege at Blue Mountain*.

Confrontation between Cutter and Rayek — pencil drawing used as a promotional piece for the Berkley publication of *Journey to Sorrow's End*.

Cover for the 1982 program book for the Inconjunction convention
held — where else? — near Indianapolis.

The elves get into the act: Warp's Christmas card for 1981.

From the cover of *Elf Wars*, a supplement booklet for the Elfquest role-playing game.

WENDY ©85 PINI

WENDY ©85 PINI

WENDY ©85 PINI

Convention sketches.

Costume ideas for Cutter — (top) for the Blue Mountain sequence in *Elfquest*; (bottom) for *Siege at Blue Mountain*. When readers saw the *Siege* sketches (which were admittedly only first ideas) they thought the elves had gone punk!

Before...

...and after. Ideas for tee-shirt designs.

All together now! A gathering of most of the females of *Elfquest*.

The Woman Wolfriders
and their sisters, and cousins, and friends, and...
by Deborah Dunn

This article, in shortened form, was originally written in 1981 and covered only the material that appeared in the Warp Graphics editions of *Elfquest* through issue #10. It first saw print in *The Heroines Showcase* #19, published in 1983 by The Comics Heriones Fan Club, P.O. Box 1329, Campbell, California 95009. A list of currently available back issues of T.C.H. Fan Club publications may be had by sending a stamped, self-addressed envelope to the address above. Thanks to Steven Johnson, publisher of *The Heroines Showcase*; and especially to Deby Dunn, for updating this piece on short notice.

Six basic philosophical groups have emerged during the first twenty issues of the *Elfquest* series. (*Since* Elfquest *is an ongoing tale, there may ultimately be many more issues than twenty. This article refers to those published by Warp Graphics between 1977 and 1984. - Ed.*) These are the elves (divided into four distinct cultures: the **Wolfriders**, the **Sun Folk**, the **Go-Backs**, and the "High Ones" or **Gliders** of Blue Mountain), the humans, and the trolls. At this point let me say a few words about each.

The first two elfin groups tend to be close to the earth. Natural cycles are an intimate part of their lives. The Wolfriders were the first elves introduced, and their ranks provide most of the major characters throughout the series.

As their name implies, Wolfriders ride great wolves. They are hunters who come from a primeval woodland, and who are very much in contact with the paradoxical forces of life and death in the natural world. Everyone in the tribe hunts, except for pregnant women, and those with the very youngest of children. Yet rather than making them vicious killers, the Wolfriders' way of life reinforces an intense love of life and living. The Wolfriders are also close to their bodies and the sensual world, and much is made of their trust of their instincts. The night is their time, and physical exercise their joy.

The second elf tribe to be introduced, the Sun Folk, lives at Sorrow's End, an isolated village in the desert. They also look to the earth for their way of life. The Sun Folk are farmers, however. Their lives focus on different earth cycles, primarily those of day and night, and the seasons.

The sun is their great symbol, the day is their time, and their activities tend to be mental rather than physical. They value the arts and elfin magic more than the Wolfriders do.

The third and fourth elf races are a startling contrast to the first two. The elves of Blue Mountain, the Gliders, claim to be the High Ones, the original elves to set foot upon the World of Two Moons, and the ancestors of all the other tribes. Like the Sun Folk, they have isolated themselves from what they consider to be a dangerous world. However, that isolation has been carried to such an extreme that it has proved to be nearly genocidal. Only a select few of these elves have ever left Blue Mountain. The rest are completely cut off from the natural world outside. Their great magical powers are wasted in a semi-utopian — or dystopian — society that is utterly devoid of love or creativity. Many of the Gliders, like the one called Door, have become so completely at one with their functions that they have ceased to exist as we understand the concept. This emotional barrenness is aptly symbolized by the fact that no children have been born in Blue Mountain for centuries.

Through a glass darkly...

Like the Wolfriders, the Go-Backs of the far northern mountains are a tribe at war with hostile neighbors. They are a hardy race of fighters who ride great elk-like beasts. Constant battle has hardened them into a callous distortion of the close-knit Wolfrider clan. The Go-Backs have little patience with any way of life other than their own. For magic and the arts they show only scorn. Their rough-and-ready comeraderie is open only to those who fight as skillfully as themselves.

Wolfriders and Sun Folk compliment each other. Each group alone has fine qualities that are nonetheless sharply limited in expression. The Wolfriders are strong and vigorous, but for the most part lack the use of magical powers. The Sun Folk possess much ancient wisdom, but are far from being full participants in the life of the physical. The encounters between the two tribes continues to be an enriching and horizon expanding experience for all.

Neither the Go-Backs nor the Gliders are able to accept the idea of change. They stubbornly keep to their own ways, rejecting outside influences. At times, this second pair of elf tribes seems for form a distorted reflection of the first pair. The heartless Go-Backs are to the Wolfriders what the sterile "High Ones" are to the Sun Folk: a warning of what the more vital groups might have become had they not had the courage to accept and learn from their differences.

By contrast, we humans tend at first to come off looking much less nice. At least in the beginning, *Elfquest*'s humans seem to represent all that humanity likes least about itself. Following the dictates of an intolerant religion into endless racial warfare with the Wolfriders, the humans early on the story would like nothing better than to practice genocide and have the world to themselves again. Dirty, brutal, strong rather than smart, superstitious rather than religious — as seen through the eyes of the elves — they are at once terrifying and impotent, blindly hating the elves yet unable to do them any lasting harm. Humans fear the world around them (hence their concept of numerous nature spirits which at best are disinterested in human affairs), while still wishing to regard it as their own.

This dismal initial picture of humanity has lightened in later issues of the story. A new side to the humans emerged in issue #7 (*all issue numbers refer to the original Warp Graphics editions - Ed.*) as we saw a human couple spared by the elves. In #8, another young human couple,

Nonna and Adar, embrace the astounding assumption that elves are not demons but godlings. They treat their elfin guests as objects of veneration and openly confess the humility they feel in the presence of the elves' beauty and grace. In #9, the humans' chief, Olbar the Mountain-Tall, shows the ability to face his superstitious fear and conquer it. Thus a new way of humans relating to the elves began.

Finally, there are the trolls, whom the elves seem to regard as only fractionally better than humans (and the trolls seem to return the sentiment). Sometimes it seems that the best thing one can say about the trolls, in fact, is that they are not humans! By the end of the series, however, we learn that the enmity between elves and trolls is ancient indeed. An alliance between the trolls and the elves proves short lived because of their insurmountable differences.

The trolls are, by our standards, phenomenally ugly; this applies to their personalities as well as to their warty hides. Their only emotions seem to be lust and greed, with fear thrown in upon occasion. Trolls are tried and true materialists. To them, love is a matter of wealth. "Any troll worth his hammer knows that a maiden's love is as true as the gold he gives her," the troll Picknose tells us in issue #7, "and the more gold, the more true her love." Trolls live in underground caverns, trading wrought metal goods and weapons to the elves in exchange for fresh meat and hides. Like the elves of Blue Mountain, they have cut themselves off from contact with the natural world. The brilliance of sunlight is more than they can endure.

Again, humans and trolls seem to reflect each others' characteristics. The humans of Olbar's tribe make the first clumsy efforts to understand the elves, while the trolls reject the idea of any lasting alliance, choosing to keep to their own greedy and despotic ways. For the humans there is a hope of a better, less contentious future; but the trolls have condemned themselves to perpetual darkness.

The above sketches are great generalizations, of course. Each of *Elfquest*'s characters is an individual, acting as such. Time has wrought changes for all of them, some more than others. One of the Wolfriders, Rainsong, has become almost like one of the Sun Folk. Others, like Moonshade, continue to display a mild disdain for the peaceful ways of the desert dwellers. Most of the Wolfriders have managed to preserve their cultural integrity while keeping open minds toward the Sun Folk, attempting to learn from differences and similarities. Even trolls and humans are sometimes presented in a light which makes their unfriendly actions comprehensible, if not acceptable. There have been good humans and evil elves. This depth and variety of characterization is what gives *Elfquest* its special impact.

The main focus of *Elfquest*, within the context of these six groups, is on characters, and especially characters in relationships. The many and varied relationships, with their parallels and sudden interminglings, are the heart of *Elfquest*. Parents and children. Friends, male and female. Lovers, mated or otherwise. There are more mated couples, family groups and close tribal societies in *Elfquest* than in the rest of comicdom put together. The story at first focused on the Wolfriders, especially the two best buddies, Cutter and Skywise. The story then expands to include the first encounters withe the Sun Folk, and Cutter's courtship of Leetah, his lifemate-to-be. (Let us pause for a moment at this point to talk about "marriage". Marriage in *Elfquest* jargon is called "lifemating", which

A new look at elves, and a leap of faith.

Roles - an early view:
Sun Villager vs. Wolfrider.

ought to say something about the kind of relationship elfin society is based upon. None of this equal-but-not-quite-equal husband-and-wife business for them! Both partners are truly equal in lifemating, a bond that means exactly what it sounds like. Lifemates mate for life, with all the long-term commitment that so often seems lacking in modern marriages.) Later in the saga the action grows again to include Cutter's quest for answers about who and what the elves were and are. The entire tale can be viewed as an expanding series of relationships.

But, putting aside the philosophical implications of Cutter's quest, and getting to the particular subject of this article, let's look at some of the common character types that appear in the series' development. First, there are the female leaders who appear among the Sun Folk, trolls, humans, Gliders and Go-Backs. Each one of these figures is central to what we know of the tribal group, and to how we feel about it.

Primary among these is Savah, Mother of Memory to the Sun Folk. I like the title "Mother of Memory" because it describes Savah's function so well. She is the keeper of lore and history for her tribe, their greatest magician, and (almost literally) the mother of them all as one of the two women from whom the entire tribe is descended. Savah is a living symbol of the past, and a focus for the emotions of her tribe. Even the eldest of them can find a mother and wise counselor in her, if they so need. Her magical powers are all but forgotten by the tribe, but the wisdom of a very long life is available, through her. Savah seems to assume this role, not as a social custom, but out of her own personal aptitude and choice. Often she helps the Sun Folk wrestle with their problems, and when an explanation of something is needed, everyone immediately turns to Savah. Without her, the Sun Folk are virtually helpless.

Savah's counterpart among the trolls is Maggoty, and her name tells it all. Maggoty is not quite as ancient to her small tribe of three as Savah is to the Sun Folk, yet in her distorted way she does mirror Savah's role with them. Maggoty is the oldest of the remaining forest trolls (the rest of their group lost a war and got marched away to the frozen north). She keeps most of their remaining lore and history, and all of the "magic" (actually, herb lore) is hers. It is Maggoty who mixes up the sleeping powders the trolls use to subdue their foes, and who brews up the wonderful concoction called dreamberry wine. Maggoty is a reflection of the differences between elves and trolls in that she does not advise people what to do. No, she *tells* them, and her orders are generally obeyed (or else!).

A third female leader is the Bone Woman, whose rule of terror over the human tribe of Olbar the Mountain-Tall ends in issue #9. Like many of *Elfquest*'s humans, the Bone Woman seems to represent a negative extreme. Like Savah of the Sun Folk, she is a spiritual leader. But with the worst impulses of a religious institution, she uses her influence to maintain her power rather than enlighten her people. What knowledge she possesses is carefully kept to herself, to be used to her own best advantage. Though in magical terms she is far from a charlatan (her totemic bones do "speak" to her), much of her power, like Maggoty's, is concentrated in herbal preparations and a clever use of drugs. Unlike Maggoty, however, the Bone Woman manipulates instead of threatening. She is a very dangerous character, and her motives are very clear to the reader. She is greedy and selfish, but at the root of her dealings with the elves is the impulse for survival that motivates her. Her bones have warned her that the elves will be her downfall. Acting on this information she actually creates her own fall from grace. But while we may disapprove of her actions, can any of us deny the reasoning behind them?

Winnowill of Blue Mountain is undoubtedly the most perplexing of all the characters in the series. The only other who even comes close to her is Two-Edge, her half-breed son. Like Two-Edge, Winnowill may be mad, but it is difficult to tell. If so, it is a dreadful madness, all the more because on the surface she seems completely sane.

Winnowill is not, throughout the original story, actually the leader of the self-named High Ones, yet her actions dominated the second half of the series. Some of *Elfquest's* readers have compared her to Adolf Hitler, and not without reason. Winnowill possesses great healing powers, which she uses in a negative way to torture other elves. At one point she captures Savah's spirit and holds her prisoner for no reason except, it seems, to revel in her ability to do so. Winnowill has a cunning mind and an intensely magnetic personality. Her skill at manipulating others puts the Bone Woman's efforts to shame. She can attain anything she wants, whether by menacing, cajoling, or seducing.

The Go-Back way —
thick skins and blunt talk.

Winnowill's motives are never clear. At times she professes to be motivated by concern for Lord Voll, the titular leader of the Gliders. At other times she speaks of him almost with contempt. Confronted by Leetah, whose own healing powers could have restored her twisted mind, Winnowill chooses to leap from a nearly fatal height. She is a character whose psychological depths have yet to be explored, and she remains a powerful, fascinating enigma.

Finally there is Kahvi, chieftess of the Go-Backs. Her function is to lead her tribe in battle, and she does this very well. Kahvi is gutsy and outspoken but, like all her people, lacks subtlety and compassion. When One-Eye of the Wolfriders is killed by trolls, her only comment is that now his widow will be a better fighter. Kahvi nearly leaves Cutter for dead on the battlefield as well, but the Wolfriders insist otherwise.

In her own way, Kahvi is as bigoted as the trolls. It seems that a lifetime of endless fighting has worn all the softness out of her, leaving only rough edges. She never wastes sympathy, even on herself. Kahvi does whatever she has to to get her tribe to do what she wants, even resorting to mockery or blows. It is this that sets her as a leader so clearly apart from Cutter, whom she otherwise seems much like. The Wolfrider chief rarely must force his will on anyone in his tribe. Among the Wolfriders, even at the worst times, decisions are made by concensus. But the Go-Backs do things differently, and nowhere are those differences more plainly seen than in the personalities of the two leaders.

There is a certain category of heroine in popular literature with whom we are all familiar: the princess. Almost invariably, she is a helpless creature of delicate disposition, daughter of the local king (or duke, or what have you). She is the most stunningly beautiful woman alive and, incidentally, the male protagonist's love interest. She would be no one if she were not connected to some man (first her father, then her paramour) and her greatest talents lie in fainting, being captured, and/or dying. It's disquieting. Fortunately, there are none of these in *Elfquest*. The few female characters who start out looking like they might be princesses end up being something else entirely.

Among trolls, Maggoty's granddaughter Oddbit is the Most Beautiful Woman. To us, she would seem almost unbearably ugly, with a huge frame, a nose like a limp sausage, a tiny, weak chin, warty skin, and small, squinty eyes. But to trolls, Oddbit is the most gorgeous creature in the world, and she knows it. She flaunts it, believing herself inviolable. She flirts unmercifully with the last surviving (she believes) male troll, her suitor Picknose, giggling, fluttering her eyelashes, cuddling up to him, and lounging with elephantine seductiveness. She is a great source of comic relief.

One is always aware of her canny mind beneath that preposterous beauty, however. It soon becomes clear to everyone, except for poor old Picknose, that she is only playing with him. Oddbit has no intention of marrying Picknose, even though he is literally the "last man on earth", unless and until he makes himself the World's Richest Troll. Nothing less will content this most practical of damsels. And indeed, it is not until the end of the quest, when Picknose becomes king of the trolls, that she gives in to him.

Oddbit's elfin counterpart is Leetah, Cutter's lifemate, the healer of the Sun Village, and daughter of the Suntoucher (the Sun Village's "high priest"). Just as Oddbit is Maggoty's granddaughter, so is Leetah descended from Savah. All these relationships do not define her character, however. They merely underline her crucial position.

In many ways, Leetah is the most complex and important of *Elfquest's* female characters. Time and again the entire course of events pivots upon what Leetah does or does not do. The fact that she is not a simple character enhances her role, for one can never be certain what she will do. Part of the difficulty in understanding Leetah's actions is that she doesn't always behave in a rational, logical manner. In this she is much like most of us.

When we first see her in *Elfquest* #2 Leetah is flirting with Rayek, her first suitor in a manner much like Oddbit's, although Leetah seems to be dangling Rayek more for the sake of fun than to get anything out of him. Then, out of the blue, Cutter and the Wolfriders come swooping down upon the Sun Village. Compelled by Recognition, an irresible mating urge, Cutter abducts Leetah.

Leetah — a personality in flux.

This is the first of several shocks for Leetah. Like many modern women who believe themselves to be independent and "liberated", Leetah discovers that her society simply has not prepared her to defend herself in a crisis situation. Captured by the Wolfriders, she is incapable of doing anything more than to scream, "Rayek, do something!" Yet when Rayek is threatened, she folds like a house of cards and offers to do anything the Wolfriders ask to save him. And, again, as soon as Cutter sets her down, she takes command, giving orders in the tone of an equal or superior. Clearly she very much likes to be in control of herself, and when control is taken out of her hands, she is at a loss.

How can we explain all of these changes, and those that followed? It has been said that only in fiction are human beings expected to act in a reasonable manner. Only the best writing recognizes the essential changeability of human nature, and can portray it in a coherent form. Like most of us at one time or another, Leetah does not always act rationally. At the same time, however, she never behaves as she does without a reason.

The key to understanding Leetah's personality is her love of freedom and her need of a stable base for her life. In a normal situation, where all is as it has been for centuries, Leetah is a confident, fearless person. But in an abnormal situation, or one in which her freedom is threatened, she either freezes up or acts irrationally. It takes several issues before

Elfquest's readers are allowed to see Leetah in a normal, nonthreatening situation, and so until then we do not see her at her best.

The greatest threat to Leetah's freedom and her life order is her Recognition of Cutter. Recognition is another, particularly significant, piece of *Elfquest* lore. Briefly, Recognition is a genetically specialized form of love at first sight, taking place between two genetically ideal elves, binding them together in an intense, irresistible fashion for the purpose of producing extraordinary offspring. Once Recognized, the two elves cannot refuse each other, for if they do not mate, they will become deathly ill without each other.

Cutter the Wolfrider never questions Recognition, but Leetah does, resisting to the point where Cutter begins to fear death. Leetah's horrified denial of Recognition is perhaps understandable to us, because most modern readers don't much go for the idea of biological predestination. To Leetah, Recognition is a deadly threat, both to her stable life and to her freedom to make her own decisions. It is the greatest challenge of her life to make a place in it for Cutter, and it takes four issues for her to accept Recognition as part of the natural order, and not a violation thereof.

Leetah's next great challenge begins in issue #8. After Cutter embarks upon the quest named in the series' title, Leetah learns through Savah and her own son, Suntop, that Cutter is advancing toward a great, nameless danger. Savah has expended all of her psychic strength to obtain the meager warning, and has implanted it in Suntop's mind, from which place only Cutter can release it. Leetah therefore has no choice but to venture into the vast, unknown world outside Sorrow's End, so that Cutter and Suntop may be reunited and the danger made clear. If she refuses to leave her home, she knows that Cutter may die.

We never see Leetah's struggle to decide whether or not to leave the comfort and security of Sorrow's End, the only place she has ever lived in all her life. From our knowledge of her, we can imagine this well enough. What we do see is that courageous moment when she leaves her home to seek and warn her lifemate. In the wide desert she faces the terror of the elements and finds that reality, though fearsome, is not really as bad as she had feared. The danger she imagined is more terrifying than reality itself.

Midway through issue #9, the skeletal remains of a solitary elf are discovered at the desert's edge. Leetah believes them to be those of Rayek, her former suitor and dearest friend. To her surprise, she discovers that the shock and grief do not kill her. From them, as from her fear, she draws the strength to turn away and continue her journey. And in issue #10, when she finally reaches both Cutter and the dreaded forest, she at last asks to be taught how to be a Wolfrider, so she may move through the woods competently and meet the forest on its own terms.

Leetah faces many challenges in the issues that follow, but these are the ones that first try her character. The strength that she finds in meeting them sustain her through all other dangers.

There are a number of other interesting women characters who do not fall so easily into categories. For the sake of simplicity, I'll discuss them by racial groups, starting with the Sun Folk.

As mentioned earlier, *Elfquest* features a number of prominent family groups. The most significant of these in the Sun Village is Leetah's, which includes her parents, and her sister. Toorah, Leetah's mother, is a delightful lady, as settled in life as Leetah, and of a greater serenity. She

At last, the acceptance of Recognition.

is close to her two adult daughters, yet not above teasing them at times. Toorah is also keenly aware of the purpose of the Sun Village as a human-free haven. Although she accepts her daughter's departure with as much grace as she can muster, it is clear she does not approve. Disapproval, however, only makes her concern show more clearly. It cannot banish her love for her daughter.

Leetah's sister is called Shenshen, and in their way the sisters are strikingly alike. Shenshen is lighthearted without being empty-headed, and she continues to enjoy the company of men, just as Leetah did before Cutter's arrival. She, too, has a personal skill — that of midwifery, a gift appropriately close to Leetah's healing. She relishes using her gift, just as Leetah enjoys healing, or perhaps even more, since she has few chances to employ it (elves have a very low birthrate). Sometimes antagonizing, sometimes teasing, almost always affectionate, Shenshen has had a rich relationship with her sister, and is a major supporting character, representing, perhaps, the Sun Folk at their most open and engaging.

There is also a trio of lovely ladies who are frequently to be seen with the dashing Skywise. After all, what's a comic book without some fellow who has women dripping off him all the time? In this case, his sex appeal is so exaggerated that it is impossible to take offense. Remarkably, there is never any animosity shown among Skywise's three paramours. Rather, they seem to have an informal agreement to share Skywise among themselves equally, enjoying him for what he is, rather than trying to possess him. This is a remarkably sensible attitude for them to take, considering how unlikely it is that Skywise will ever settle down.

Among humans, a grand total of four women (named, not background) characters have appeared. This places them just above the trolls, who are stuck at two. Of these four, the Bone Woman has already been mentioned. The first to appear as an actual character in the series was Thaya (*Elfquest*#6). She is an outcast travelling through the desert with nothing but her husband, her son, her crazed brother-in-law and a pony. She plays mostly a supporting role to her husband, Aro, which is not surprising given the society she comes from.

The third human woman, who first appeared in Marvel Comics' *Epic Illustrated* #1 and who entered the main *Elfquest* saga in issue #9, is Selah, daughter of Olbar the Mountain-Tall. She is another princess type who breaks out of the mold. Though not an important character, she has been consistently interesting. As befits the daughter of a great chieftain, she is strong-willed and relatively fearless, carrying a flint knife and willing to use it. She is also first seen running away with her lover, whom her father despises because he failed his test of manhood. What better guarantee is there of reader sympathy?

Most important of the human women is Nonna. She and her husband, Adar, lived alone in the forest until Cutter and Skywise helped them regain admission to Olbar's village in issue #9. Like Leetah, Nonna is (in her own quiet way) a healer, and like Savah, she dispenses a certain amount of lore as a symbol-maker. Yet unlike Thaya's people, she has been raised to accept the presence of elves (which she considers "spirits") in the world without panic. In later issues she even begins to lead Olbar's people toward her own reverent view of the elves.

Discovering Cutter in a fevered delirium, Nonna takes him in and attempts to cure him as she would a human child (*Elfquest* #8). This particularly alarms Skywise. There is a certain amount of hostility and

Humans *can* be kind.

confusion before the elves can accept the concept of friendly, helpful humans. Even when Nonna's good intentions have been proven, Cutter and Skywise have difficulty believing them. Yet it is her friendship that is crucial to both their quest and to the humans' change of attitude in issue #9.

Only one female character aside from Winnowill stands out among the Blue Mountain elves. This is Aroree, one of the Chosen Eight. She serves as a hunter for her people, riding a huge hawklike bird and bringing in captured game. Of all her people, only Aroree is open enough to reach out to the Wolfriders. She quickly becomes friends with Skywise, but is not able to escape the strictures of her society completely. Aroree is a troubled character, torn between her attraction to Skywise and her loyalty to Blue Mountain.

Likewise, only one Go-Back woman besides Kahvi really emerges as a character in her own right, and her story strangely parallels Aroree's. This is Vaya, a young warrior who becomes friends with Pike during the Wolfriders' stay with the Go-Backs. Her relationship with Kahvi is strained, however. The chieftess is especially hard on Vaya; nothing the girl does ever seems to be good enough. During the assault on the northern trolls' mountain fortress at the end of the quest, Vaya is captured, tortured and killed. Only after her death do the Wolfriders learn that she was Kahvi's daughter.

Finally, we come to the women Wolfriders named in the title of this article. Despite the importance of the other elfin cultures, the Wolfriders remain the central group in *Elfquest*, supplying almost every major character throughout the series. In all, there are seven — hunters, lovers, mothers — plus several others mentioned as being deceased. Since the Wolfriders are a small, closed group, the incidence of interrelationships among them is high. This contributes to the atmosphere of extreme emotional closeness among the Wolfriders, and explains the fact that not a woman among them can be found who is not actively participating in at least one relationship of some kind.

The first woman, human or elfin, seen in *Elfquest* is Nightfall, and in my eyes she remains the most important of the woman Wolfriders. In many ways, Nightfall represents the very best that the Wolfriders can produce. She is strong and independent, giving an unshakable love to her lifemate Redlance. Often, one discovers, love to the Wolfriders means protection of the beloved, be it parent, child, sibling or mate. Just so, Nightfall insists upon remaining with her injured Redlance in the desert to defend him (*Elfquest* #2) even though there is a good chance this will mean her own death. Nightfall is also the first and almost only Wolfrider to reach out to Leetah during her struggle with Recognition, to try to help and understand. Later, she speaks in Leetah's defense before less tolerant Wolfriders. Knowing herself and her own value, Nightfall is not afraid to reach out to others. She has more courage than most, elf or modern human.

Each of the other characters is just as much an individual, with distinct strengths and weaknesses. Dewshine is Cutter's cousin, daughter of his mother's brother. She is perhaps best known for her skinny, flat-chested build (it is ironic that a comic book character should be considered unique for having an *un*-buxom body), but is a lively young lady nonetheless. Forever to be found at the forefront of hunt and battle, she risks her life with impetuous delight.

Clearbrook is the eldest of the female Wolfriders, and was the lifemate

Nightfall — a wellspring of love... and loving strength.

117

of One-Eye, who perished during the troll battles in the bitter mountains of the north. Taken in by the Go-Backs, she falls into a maniacal blood-lust, wanting nothing but revenge against the trolls. By the end of the series, however, a measure of peace has returned to her.

Rainsong is the Total Mother among the Wolfriders; the soft and retiring one who becomes so much at home among the Sun Folk. She devotes her entire being to the care of her family in a way that somehow transcends the stereotypical.

Moonshade seems to represent the "straight" Wolfrider, with the fierce love of her people, but less of their openness. Though certainly not an evil character, she is not always entirely positive. She is too much a Wolfrider, unwilling or unable to open her mind to the ways of the Sun Folk. Though she has lived in the Sun Village and knows their way of life, Moonshade does not truly respect it. To her, the Wolfriders' way is the only way, and her impatience with Leetah on a number of occasions only underscores this intolerance.

Timmain is the ancient ancestress of the Wolfriders who suddenly — and shockingly — reveals herself to them at the very end of the series. A true High One, Timmain long ago took the form of a she-wolf and has lived as one for thousands of years. Although she can acknowledge the Wolfriders as her descendants, Timmain is not one of them. Her stay among them is too brief for that. She reveals the secrets of their past to the elves and then seals herself away forever within the palace that was the origin place of the High Ones. It seems only fitting, since she has been so much a part of the past, that she at the last join it physically as well.

Another woman Wolfrider, whose influence continues to be felt even after her death, is the chieftess Joyleaf, Cutter's mother. Actually, both of Cutter's parents were significant people. Their relationship was one of ideal mutual completion. Bearclaw, the chief, lived with a flair for enjoying the present that is typical of the Wolfriders, especially before the destruction of their forest home in issue #1. He gambled, drank, and stole the humans' children for sport. Joyleaf was exactly his opposite, a quiet person who knew how to enjoy life without being active every moment. Her specialty was wisdom, and her major task was restraining Bearclaw's hatred of humans. Together Bearclaw and Joyleaf created balance and order for the Wolfriders and themselves — no small task.

One last class of characters that is virtually unique to *Elfquest* is the children, generally a forgotten minority in comics (which is truly ironic, since children are comics' readers, at least in theory!). *Elfquest* regularly features five children, more than can be found anywhere else except the pages of *Richie Rich*. They are, not necessarily in order of importance, Suntop and Ember (Cutter and Leetah's twins), Wing and Newstar (Rainsong's two children), and Dart (son of Moonshade). All of them are portrayed with that mixture of innocence and wisdom typical of all but the youngest of children, and all possess the bouncy self-assurance of children who never doubt they are loved.

The farther I progress with this article, the more I realize the futility of trying to talk about *Elfquest* without talking about its men. It's true, a few names have crept in here and there: Cutter. Skywise. Redlance. Picknose. Rayek. Fascinating names for fascinating characters. I'd like to give them the attention they deserve.

Unfortunately, I have to place a limit somewhere; one article can cover only so much. The male characters are a whole different barrel of

Joyleaf — a moderating influence.

monkeys, and this *is* about the females of *Elfquest*. Still, I hope it is clear that even though there are more, and better, women in *Elfquest* than in ten issues of the next best comic book title — and that is definitely not a statement I make lightly — no reading of *Elfquest* could ever be complete that did not take into account the men.

Having said this, I can go on to point out one final thing that, I think, accounts for the ultimate appeal of *Elfquest*. That is its treatment of the characters. A comic, or any other book, can have characters of every conceivable sort, but they would all be cardboard cutouts without the author's respect for each and every one of them. In a letter to me, Richard Pini wrote, "...it's not so much a case of sitting down one day and plotting it (*Elfquest*) as it is a case of knowing each and every character intimately and letting the story flow." It is that kind of care that makes *Elfquest* what it is.

With all the odd-type people in *Elfquest*, the men and women, the children and old people, the elves, trolls and humans, there is hardly one of them that the reader doesn't come to know and respect as a person. The cast of *Elfquest* includes a tremendous variety, and yet each character is valued for what he or she is. Thus the full range of human experience and feeling, good, bad and neutral, is acknowledged and approved. To be fully human is to have something of each character in us, and there is nothing wrong in that.

The "message" of *Elfquest*, if one must have one, is simply that very examination of the human character, in all of its manifestations. It is the recognition that this variety makes humanity what it is. *Elfquest* is about being human — what it means, how we do it, and maybe, just a little, an idea of what humanity could mean and be.

119

The
Elfquest Glossary
(part two)

Being an extension and amplification of the glossary
which appeared in Volume One, and containing more than
twice as many terms. Sincere thanks and appreciation go
to **John C. LaRue, Jr.**, **Katerina M. Hodge**, **Benjamin
Urrutia**, **Vince Mora**, **Eliann Fensvoll**, **Brad Johnson**,
and **Linda Woeltjen** for their research, and without whose
help this version of the glossary could not have been done.

A

Adar: human; exiled member of Olbar's tribe; mate to Nonna

age-mate: a friend of about the same age

Ahdri: elf; one of the Sun Folk; Savah's handmaiden

airwalker: used to refer to one who levitates, particularly to Rayek

Alekah: elf; Sun Villager; Savah's grand-daughter; a rock-shaper who formed the Sun Symbol at the end of the Bridge of Destiny

allo: a large, carnivorous dinosaur, packs of which still roam the world

always now, the: the state of mind that exists in a perpetual present; the "now of wolf thought"

anti-healing: the opposite of healing, the power to inflict pain; used by Winnowill

Aro: human; one of the refugees who came upon Sorrow's End; driven away by the Wolfriders

Aroree: elf; one of the Gliders who inhabit Blue Mountain; one of the Chosen Eight

arrow-whip: a device that uses a sling attached to a flexible stick to hurl an arrow; used by Dart in the Sun Village

Ayooooah!: a general tribal cry of the Wolfriders

Ayooah-yoh!: one of a number of special howls; specifically, "Paging Scouter!"

Aroree
(with Petalwing)

B

bagfrog: a large frog with an air-pouch at its throat

barbarian: Sun Folk term for the Wolfriders; used particularly by Leetah and Rayek to refer to Cutter

bearberry: an edible berry used by the Wolfriders to supplement their diet

Bearclaw: elf; Cutter's father; tenth chief of the Wolfriders; killed by Madcoil

beesweets: preserver term for flowers

bellow torches: used by the trolls to heat their forges to high temperature

Berrybuzz: a preserver; "leader" of the preservers after Petalwing remained at the Palace at Quest's End

big belly pictures: fertility symbols

Big Moon: the larger of the two moons that orbit the world; has a period of roughly 16 days; also called Greater Moon, Mother Moon

bigthing: preserver term for a human

"birdbasket": preserver term for a bird's nest

bird elf: Wolfrider term referring to Tyldak

bird-riders: Wolfrider term referring generally to the Chosen Eight of the Gliders

Bird Spirits: term used by Nonna and her tribe to refer to the Gliders

Blackfell: Bearclaw's wolf

black hair: Wolfrider term referring to Rayek

black snake: Wolfrider term referring to Winnowill

Blood of Ten Chiefs: honorific used in referring to Cutter

Blue Mountain: tall, solitary peak to the west of the original holt and the Forbidden Grove; home to the Gliders for thousands of years

bond-bird: used to describe the great hawks ridden by the Chosen Eight

bonding: the process by which an elf and an animal become attuned to each other, not as master and subordinate, but as equals; technically, only the Wolfriders, by virtue of their wolf blood, are truly bonded to their wolves

Bone Woman: human; former shamaness of Olbar's tribe; current whereabouts are unknown

bow-harp: a musical instrument based on a hunting bow but with more than one string

Brace: elf; Gliders; a rock-shaper, his singular function is to sense faults in the rock of Blue Mountain and to correct them

the Bone Woman

branch-horn: a deerlike animal with spreading antlers

Bridge of Destiny: a natural rock formation at Sorrow's End; a great arch that is the site of the Test of Heart (see **Trial of Hand, Head and Heart**)

Briersting: Strongbow's wolf

brightmetal: a light, strong alloy created by the trolls; New Moon is made of it

bristle-boar: a desert-dwelling pig

Bristlebrush: Scouter's wolf

Brownberry: elf; a Wolfrider; killed in the first attack by Madcoil

Brownskin: name used by the Go-Backs and Ekuar in referring to Rayek

Bruga: human; one of the Gatara tribe

bug: term used by Cutter to refer to Petalwing

"Bumper": affectionate nickname given by Scouter and Dewshine to Windkin

Burning Waste: Wolfrider term for the great desert between the Tunnel of Golden Light and Sorrow's End

burrowers: the original chimp-like creatures that evolved into the trolls

"busyhead highthing": Petalwing's term for Cutter

C

cave slugs: wormlike creatures living in the troll caverns; trolls consider them a delicacy

Challenge Wand: a carved, wooden baton, pointed at one end, bearing the images of a hand, a head, and a heart; used by rivals for the affections of a potential mate to challenge each other to the Trial of Hand, Head and Heart

Chiad G'Cho: human, one of the Hoan G'Tay Sho

chief-friend: term of affection used by Nightfall (and others) to refer to Cutter

chief's lock: a bound "ponytail" worn only by the chief of the Wolfriders

challenge wand

Child Moon: the smaller of the two moons that orbit the world; it has a period of roughly 8 days; also called Lesser Moon or Little Moon

child's teeth: seeds similar to kernels of corn, planted as a crop in Sorrow's End

Choplicker: Ember's wolf-friend

Chosen Eight, the: elves; the Gliders who ride the giant hawks from Blue Mountain; they are the providers for the entire population of Gliders

clap rocks: a musical instrument played during festivals at Sorrow's End

Clearbrook: elf; a Wolfrider; lifemate of One-Eye; mother of Scouter

clearstone: a mica-like mineral used by the Sun Folk as ornamentation

cloud tree: a desert plant whose blossoms resemble puffs of smoke

Coneheads: informal term used to refer to the natural aspect of the High Ones (with their elongated skulls) before they took the form of elves

council: a formal meeting of all the Wolfriders, usually to consider a major decision

cub: affectionate term for a Wolfrider youngster

cubling: affectionate term for a very young Wolfrider

Cutter: elf; eleventh and current chief of the Wolfriders; son of Bearclaw and Joyleaf; lifemate to Leetah; father to Suntop and Ember; called Kinseeker by Two-Edge during the Quest

D

Dark Sister: term used by Winnowill to refer to Leetah

Dart: elf; a Wolfrider; son of Strongbow and Moonshade; during the Quest remained at Sorrow's End as its protector

daystar: Sun Village term for the sun

death sleep: Wolfrider term for the season of autumn

Cutter

Death Water: the waterfall near Olbar's tribe over which the Great River flows into the Valley of Endless Sleep

"deer-sloth": Scouter's name for a zwoot

demons: human term for elves

den-hide: command for all Wolfriders in the area to make themselves as invisible as possible to avoid detection by an enemy

Dewshine: elf; a Wolfrider; daughter of Treestump and Rillfisher; cousin to Cutter; lovemate to Scouter; mother of Windkin by Recognition with Tyldak

"dig-digs": preserver term for trolls

Door: elf; a Glider; a rock-shaper, her only function is to open and close the rock wall that leads from within Blue Mountain to the tribe of the Hoan G'Tay Sho outside; also another Glider of the same function deep within Blue Mountain

double-shell nuts: an edible nut whose meat is protected within two tough shells

dreamberry: a berry native to the World of Two Moons; fresh from the bush it induces drunkenness in elves; fermented, the wine is hallucinogenic to elves; can be poisonous to humans

dreamberry talk: drunken babbling

dreamberry vision: a hallucination

dreamberry wine: fermented product of dreamberry juice; first concocted by the trolls living under the original holt, a tradition kept up by Old Maggoty

Dreen: elf; one of the Rootless Ones; a male child adopted by Hassbet

Dro: human; Aro's brother; died of illness while the humans were at Sorrow's End

E

Egg: elf; a Glider; a kind of rock-shaper, his sole function is to keep the Great Egg levitated and slowly spinning as he adds to its carvings

eight-of-days: elfin unit of time similar to a week

the effects of dreamberry wine

Ekuar: elf; a rock-shaper who escaped from the Frozen Mountain trolls; rescued by Rayek and now living with the Go-Backs

elf: one of a number of different groups of beings, all descended from the original group of High Ones, who now inhabit the World of Two Moons; most known elves (Wolfriders, Sun Folk, Go-Backs) are shorter and hardier than their forebears, though some (Gliders) are still tall and delicate

elf-friend: a wolf's particular Wolfrider

Ember: elf; a Wolfrider; daughter of Cutter and Leetah; Suntop's twin sister

"Evil Ones": human term for elves

eyes-meeting-eyes: term used by the Sun Folk to describe the moment of Recognition

Eyes of Timmorn: constellation named by Skywise; refers to two brighter stars within a dimmer cluster

F

Fahr: Skywise's soul name

fan bushes: palm-like desert plants around Sorrow's End

Father Tree: the great, hollow tree at the center of the original Holt that served as home to the Wolfriders, first shaped by Goodtree; destroyed by fire; also, the new dwelling tree within Forbidden Grove

Festival of Flood and Flower: annual celebration held by the Sun Folk at the end of the rainy season

fever dream: a delirium

Firecoat: Redlance's wolf

fire eye: gem mined by the trolls

firemaker: one whose "magic" talent is the starting of fires

firstborn: early Wolfrider name for those born of the mating between High Ones

firstcomer: early Wolfrider name for those who appeared from the Palace; same as **High One**

Ember

First Dance: the oldest of the Sun Folk celebration dances, it tells of the Rootless Ones and the founding of Sorrow's End

fisher bird: a water fowl similar to a kingfisher

"five-fingers": Wolfrider term for human

fixed star: Skywise's term for the star, which never seems to move during a night, nearest to the Hub of the Sky Wheel

flesh-shaping: an elfin "magic" power to shape flesh into any form, natural or unnatural; a kind of psychokinesis; healing is a form of flesh-shaping on the macro- or microscopic level

floater: term for an elf who has the power to levitate; slightly different from a glider, as a floater does not have the power of propulsion as well as levitation

"floods and flowerings": Sun Folk term for a year

"flyhighbaby": Petalwing's name for Windkin

"flyhighthing": Petalwing's name for Tyldak

Forbidden Grove: a dense grove west of Olbar's village and east of Blue Mountain; original home of the preservers after Winnowill sent them from Blue Mountain; feared by Olbar's tribe as the dwelling place of evil spirits

forest brothers: Wolfrider term for wolves

Foxfur: elf; Wolfrider; lovemate to Skywise at the time she was killed by Madcoil

Freefoot: elf; Wolfrider; sixth chief of the Wolfriders

Frozen Mountains: the great mountain chain that lies to the north of Blue Mountain, beyond which lies the Palace of the High Ones; home to the northern trolls

fur flower: forest plant with white, puffy petals

"fursoft cradlebaby": preserver term for a sleeping mouse

flesh-shaping
(Winnowill at work on Tyldak)

G

Geoki: human; Hoan G'Tay Sho child; became friends with Dart

127

Geru: human; one of Nonna and Adar's three adopted children

Gliders: elves who inhabit Blue Mountain; all Gliders have the power of levitation and limited, gliding flight; Gliders are generally taller than other elf groups, and are potentially immortal; led by Lord Voll until his death, they are now dominated by Winnowill

Go-Backs: elf tribe inhabiting the region just south of the Frozen Mountains; a tribe of hunters, led by Kahvi, who have given up the use of magic; they were the first to feel the "pull" of the Palace of the High Ones when it was freed from its glacial tomb

Golden Hoard: Two-Edge's name for the weapons and armor he forged; he named it thus to appeal to Picknose's greed and so manipulate the troll's actions

Goodtree: elf; Wolfrider; eighth chief of the Wolfriders; established the holt where Cutter was born

Goodtree's Rest: constellation named by Skywise

Gotara: the supreme spirit of the tribe of humans who burned the Wolfriders out of the original holt

"go out": term used when an elf (so far, only Savah, Winnowill and Suntop) travels outside his or her body in astral form

Graysha: Olbar's latest mate

Great Egg: a huge, ovoid sculpture inside Blue Mountain that contains within its many concentric layers the pictorial history of the Gliders

Great Ice Wall: Go-Back term for the glacier that, until recently, hid the Palace of the High Ones

Great River: river that flows by Olbar's camp

Great Wolf: constellation named by Skywise

Great Sky Wheel: Skywise's term for the entire sky, which seems to wheel overhead as time passes

Greater Moon: see **Big Moon**

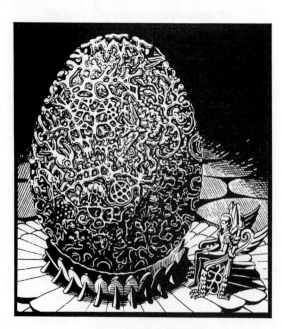

the Great Egg
(tended by Egg)

"green growing place": Leetah's term for the forest or woods in general

Greymung: king of the holt trolls until his death at the hands of the invading northern trolls

Guiders: the "coneheads" who were responsible for navigating the palace-ship on its voyage through the stars

Guttlekraw: king of the northern trolls until his death at the hands of Cutter and Kahvi during the final battle of the quest

H

Halek: elf; Sun Villager; taught by Dart to use the arrow-whip

"hand, head and heart": refers to the three tests of challenge in the Sun Village; see **Trial of Hand, Head and Heart**

"hangey-down": preserver term for a cocoon in which some living thing is encased, hanging like a pendulum from a branch

Hassbet: elf; one of the Rootless Ones; cousin to Maalvi; Savah's mother

healer: one who has healing powers

healing: the "magic" power to shape flesh to close wounds, knit bone, cleanse the body of poisons, and so on; a kind of psychokinesis

High Ones: general elfin term for the beings who first came out of the Palace when it crashed on the World of Two Moons; the ancestors of all elves

"highthing": preserver term for an elf

Hoan G'Tay Sho: humans; the tribe lives at the base of Blue Mountain and worships the Gliders; Nonna's tribe

holt: generally, any place where the Wolfriders live; particularly, their current home (**the holt**)

Holtfinder: Moonshade's wolf

holt trolls: trolls who lived beneath the Wolfriders' original forest holt; a splinter group from the northern trolls

Greymung

THE WOLFRIDERS, *TOO*, JOIN IN THE SINGING -- AND IT IS AN EERIE, HAUNTING *COMMUNION* OF *KINDRED SPIRITS!*

a howl

hood spider: a desert spider that hides under the sand

hoof-dog: a desert animal similar to a boar

Hotburr: Pike's wolf

Howl: a Wolfrider ritual; a gathering of the tribe to celebrate or mourn a person or event; there may be storytelling or simply a howl to the sky

Hub of the Great Sky Wheel: that part of the sky around which all the stars appear to rotate; the north sky pole

Human Hunter: constellation described by Skywise

human: general term used to describe the original inhabitants of the World of Two Moons; human tribes are scattered throughout the world; some groups are analogous to Neanderthal Man in evolution, some to Cro-Magnon; humans vary widely in their reactions to elves

hummer: a tiny bird with fast-beating wings

hunt, the: early Wolfrider term used to describe particularly the offspring of Timmorn and she-wolves, or any elf who had very strong wolf characteristics

Huntress Skyfire: elf; Wolfrider; fifth chief of the Wolfriders

I

Itchback: troll; one of the northern trolls killed by Cutter and Rayek before the great battle

J

jack-wolf: a hybrid of jackal and wolf; used by Dart and others in the Sun Village

Joyleaf: elf; Wolfrider; lifemate to Bearclaw; Cutter's mother; killed by Madcoil

juiceberries: succulent berries that grow in the forest

K

Kahvi: elf; Go-Back; chief of the Go-Backs; mother of Vaya and Rayek's unnamed daughter and...

Kakuk: human; a servant to Winnowill in Blue Mountain

kill-hunger: a frenzy

Kinseeker: name given by Two-Edge to Cutter

kitling: Sun Village term of affection

Kiv: elf; Go-Back

Kohahn-Chief: human; leader of the Hoan G'Tay Sho

Krim: elf; Go-Back; chose to live with the Wolfriders after Quest's End

Kureel: elf; Glider; one of the Chosen Eight

L

Land's Edge: human term for the horizon

Leetah: elf; Sun Villager; lifemate to Cutter; daughter of Suntoucher and Toorah; mother of Suntop and Ember; an accomplished healer; no longer living in Sorrow's End, Leetah is currently learning the Way of the Wolfriders

Lesser Moon: see **Child Moon**

Lifebearer: name sometimes given to Woodlock

lifemate: an elf who has consciously and freely made a commitment to another to bond for life (or at least a very long time); to make such a bond (see **lovemate**)

Lift-Leg: human; he inadvertently showed Tanner one way to cure animal hides by urinating over the pit where Tanner had buried the skins

"little star cousins": Skywise's term for fireflies

Lionskin: Treestump's wolf

Little Moon: see **Child Moon**

Littletrill: Aroree's giant hawk

lock-sending: a kind of telepathy that is closed to all but sender and recipient

Lodestone, the: the fragment of magnetic stone that Skywise wears as an amulet around

Leetah

Lord Voll

Madcoil

his neck; also, the magnetic meteorite from which the fragment came

Longbranch: elf; Wolfrider; One-Eye's brother; was called Longreach; killed by Madcoil

Longreach: old tribe name for Longbranch

Longspear: constellation named by Skywise

longtooth: a large, wild cat resembling a sabretooth

Lord Voll: elf; Glider; one of the firstborn of the group of High Ones who fled the Palace and ended up at Blue Mountain; killed by Frozen Mountain trolls

Loveless One: name used by Savah and Leetah to refer to Winnowill

lovemate: an elf who joins with another for the pleasure involved, but who has not made a stronger commitment; to engage in lovemating (see **lifemate**)

Lree: Dewshine's soul name

M

Maalvi: elf; one of the Rootless Ones; cousin to Hasbett

Madcoil: monstrous creature born of the magical mutation/combination of a giant snake and a longtooth

"magic": general term used to describe various elfin abilities or powers; not used in the supernatural sense, "magic" is actually considered to be a kind of energy which can be used and stored and refers to powers of the mind such as telekinesis, telepathy, pyrokinesis and so on

Maggoty: see **Old Maggoty**

"magic feeling": Suntop's term for the feeling he gets whenever he is around magic or a place where magic has been used

Malak: human; a youth, much disliked by Olbar, who ran away with the chief's daughter Selah

Man-Tricker: elf; Wolfrider; ninth chief of the Wolfriders

marsh-piper: a singing bird

Mekda: elf; a rock-shaper captured and mutilated by Frozen Mountain trolls and forced to dig for them; called by them Sack 'o' Bones; died of exposure during the final battle

metal shaper: one who has the power to shape more-or-less pure metals (either those that have been refined or those which are found naturally in a pure state, such as gold or copper)

midday fumes: Sun village term for the hottest part of the day

Minyah: elf; Sun Villager; a gardener who witnesses Redlance's emerging plant-shaping powers

moon madness: insanity, crazy ideas

Moonshade: elf; Wolfrider; mate to Strongbow, mother of Dart

moonsword: sometimes used to refer to New Moon because of its shape

moss mush: troll baby food

Mother of Memory, the: see **Savah**

Mother Moon: see **Big Moon**

"mountain thing": human term for the fallen Palace of the High Ones

mump: among the trolls, a youngster

N

"nastybad high dig-dig": Petalwing's name for Two-Edge

near-wolf: Cutter's term for a dog

Nestrobber: One-Eye's third wolf

new green: Wolfrider term for the season of spring

New Moon: Cutter's sword; forged by Two-Edge out of brightmetal; first owned by Bearclaw; contains the key to Two-Edge's armory

Newstar: elf; Wolfrider; daughter of Rainsong and Woodlock; currently living in Sorrow's End

Nightfall: elf; Wolfrider; lifemate to Redlance

Nightrunner: wolf; Cutter's first wolf-friend

Nightfall (and Redlance)

Nima: human; one of Nonna and Adar's three adopted children

nohump: elfin term for pony

"noisybad bubblebangs": preserver term for the explosive globes that line the tunnel within Blue Mountain leading to Winnowill's private chambers

Nonna: human; mate to Adar; symbol maker to the Hoan G'Tay Sho

northern trolls: trolls who live beneath the Frozen Mountains

"now of wolf thought": see **always now, the**

O

Oddbit

Oddbit: holt troll; Old Maggoty's granddaughter; beloved of Picknose; an opportunist of the first water

Olbar (the Mountain-Tall): human; chief of the tribe that dwells by the Great River

Old Maggoty: holt troll; Oddbit's grandmother; an ancient crone, she knows the secret of brewing dreamberry wine; discovered by Bearclaw, which alerted the Wolfriders to the existence of the trolls

One-Eye: elf; Wolfrider; lifemate to Clearbrook; father of Scouter; killed by trolls, his essence now inhabits the Palace

Orolin: a Conehead who did not self-change into elfin form; keeper of the Scroll of Colors; died when his preserver cocoon was torn

Osek: elf; a rock-shaper, captured by Frozen Mountain trolls; escaped with Ekuar and Mekda; died in the desert

owl pellets: owl vomitus; otherwise used as an expression of disgust

P

Palace: also called Palace of the High Ones, Lost Dwelling of the High Ones, and other names; the starship of the High Ones (as Coneheads) "magically" shaped to resemble a castle; crashed to the World of Two Moons, stranding the elfin High Ones there for all time

palace-ship: informal term used (mostly by the writers of Elfquest) to refer to the star-traveling vehicle of the coneheads

Petalwing: preserver; "leader" of the preservers until Quest's End, then stayed with Rayek in the Palace

Picknose: holt troll; was one of King Greymung's guardsmen; currently king of the trolls living in the Frozen Mountains

Pike: elf; Wolfrider; son of Rain the healer(outside of Recognition)

preserver: a sexless, insectlike creature created by the High Ones (as Coneheads); preservers spit a kind of webbing which preserves whatever it completely enwraps; they also have a keen directional sense and have been used as living "compasses" to find the Palace

Prey-Pacer: elf; Wolfrider; third chief of the Wolfriders; son of Rahnee the She-Wolf and Zarhan Fastfire

puckernuts: very bitter nut-like fruit; expression of distaste

punkin: a gourdlike vegetable

Q

quill pig: porcupine

R

Rahnee (the She-Wolf): elf; Wolfrider; second chief of the Wolfriders; daughter of Timmorn Yellow-Eyes and Murrel

Rain: elf; Wolfrider; a healer under Bearclaw's chieftainship; killed by Madcoil

Rainsong: elf; Wolfrider; daughter of Rain; lifemate to Woodlock; mother of Newstar, Wing, and another, as yet unnamed infant; currently living in Sorrow's End

preservers (Petalwing on left)

Picknose

Savah

Rayek: elf; Sun Villager; driven to be first in all things, he left the Sun Village when the Wolfriders arrived and he lost Leetah to Cutter; later joined the Go-Backs

Recognition: the mental/genetic imperative which drives an elfin couple to mate and produce offspring; Recognition works to bring two elves together whose genetic makeup will produce superior children; to deny the urge of Recognition is to court serious illness

Redlance: elf; Wolfrider; lifemate to Nightfall; has plant-shaping ability

Redmark: Redlance's previous tribe-name

Reevol: elf; Glider; one of the Chosen Eight

Rillfisher: elf; Wolfrider; Treestump's lifemate, killed in an accident

River god: worshipped by Olbar's tribe; said to live in the Great River

rock-shaper: one who wields the power of rock-shaping, the ability to mold the physical form of rocks and minerals (as opposed to refined metals)

Rootless Ones: name of one group of High Ones who escaped from the Palace and wandered for generations before settling at Sorrow's End

"rosynose highthing": Petalwing's name for Pike

round-ears: elfin term for humans

S

"Sack 'o' Bones": troll name for Mekda

Savah: elf; Sun Villager; also called the Mother of Memory; the spiritual leader and advisor of the Sun Folk; the eldest of the Sun Folk; can use almost all of the "magical" powers available to elves

Scouter: elf; Wolfrider; son of Clearbrook and One-Eye; lovemate to Dewshine

Scroll of Colors: a magically high-technology holographic device (Clarke's Law: Any sufficiently advanced technology is indistinguishable from magic) within the Palace that contains the entire history of the High Ones and, therefore, of the elves

Scurff: holt troll; the keeper of the door that led from the tunnels to the original Holt

seek-root: a tiny-blossomed desert flower

Selah: human; daughter of Olbar; ran away with Malak

self-shaper: one who can manipulate the material of one's own body; a very difficult kind of flesh shaping (see **flesh shaping**); Timmain was the last elf to be a self-shaper

self-without-form: Savah's term for her astral being which she can project for short distances and which can be seen as a hazy image

sending: telepathic communication between or among elves; sending can be open (general broadcast to all within range) or locked (going only to those intended — see **lock sending**); all elves have the ability to send but not all have retained the practice — Wolfriders are superb while Sun Folk have forgotten the talent; sending's range is not infinite but is determined by the skill and strength of the sender

shadow beast: human term for a wolf

She-Wolf: see **Rahnee the She-Wolf**

Shenshen: elf; Sun Villager; daughter of Suntoucher and Toorah; Leetah's sister

Shyhider: Moonshade's wolf; died in the desert

Silvergrace: Rainsong's wolf; died in the desert

"silversoft highthing": Petalwing's name for Clearbrook

six-sided stones: a game of chance played by trolls

skeleton weeds: desert plants resembling tumbleweeds

Skot: elf; Go-Back; chose to live with the Wolfriders after Quest's End

Skyfire: see **Huntress Skyfire**

skyfire storm: a lightning storm

Skywise: elf; a Wolfrider; the tribe's stargazer and Cutter's confidant

Skywise

Spirit Man

sleep dust: a powder concocted by Old Maggoty that puts animals (and, by virtue of their wolf blood, Wolfriders) into a drugged sleep

Sleeping Troll: Wolfrider name for an active volcano visible from the original Holt

Smoketreader: One-Eye's wolf

"softpretty highthing": Petalwing's name for Leetah

Sorrow's End: the desert village found by the Wolfriders after their desert trek; home to the Sun Folk; also called the Sun Village; founded by the Rootless Ones

soul name: a word/sound/concept that embodies all that an elf (particularly a Wolfrider) is, mentally and spiritually; it is both door to and contents of the innermost private core of the mind; among the Wolfriders the soul name is sacred, never to be abused; some elfin tribes (Sun Folk) do not have soul names as they do not send and therefore do not fear telepathic intrusion

Spirit Man: human; shaman of the human tribe that burned the Wolfriders from their original Holt; killed by Strongbow

Spirit Slayer: name taken by the Thief for himself before being killed by Cutter

square-eye: a goatlike animal, domesticated by some early groups of elves

squatneedle: particular kind of cactus resembling barrel cactus

Starjumper: Skywise's wolf

sticker plants: Wolfrider term for cactus

"stillquiet": preserver term for asleep

sting-tail: scorpion-like desert creature

strangleweed: a vinelike plant that can quickly ensnare and enwrap anything that gets too close to it

Strongbow: elf; Wolfrider; mate to Moonshade; father of Dart; one of the tribal elders, his skill with the bow is unsurpassed; rarely speaks aloud

Strongest Man: primitive human; was the first to kill a High One soon after the Palace landed

Sun Folk: the inhabitants of Sorrow's End (also called the Sun Village); descended from the Rootless Ones

"sun-comes (or goes) -up": elfin term for east

"sun-goes-down": elfin term for west

"sunnygold highthing": Petalwing's name for Dewshine

Sun Symbol: a carving in the rock at the far side of the Bridge of Destiny

Suntop: elf; Wolfrider; son of Cutter and Leetah; Ember's twin brother

Suntoucher: elf; Sun Villager; father of Leetah; mate to Toorah; blind, he "reads" and interprets the signs of earth and sky for the Sun Folk

Sun Village: alternate name for Sorrow's End

Sur: One-Eye's soul name

symbol maker: shamaness who uses drawings to work "magic"; Nonna's title within the Hoan G'Tay Sho

Suntop

T

taal: an elfin child's game, similar to hide and seek

taal-stick: a wand used by children playing taal to touch each other, each touch counts a point

Tabak: human; killed by Cutter as he was about to sacrifice Redlance

tall one: elfin term for human

talon-whip: Glider weapon; shaped like a three-taloned bird claw at the end of a long cord

Tam: Cutter's soul name

Tanner: elf; Wolfrider; seventh chief of the Wolfriders

Tenchi: one of Nonna and Adar's three adopted children

Tenspan: greatest of the Glider hawks; flown by Lord Voll; killed by northern trolls

Tenspan's Hall: a great chamber high in Blue Mountain, open to the outside, from which the Chosen Eight fly their hawks

Timmain (being wrapped by a preserver)

a treewee

think-do: preserver term for "magic" that is the expression of mind alone, outside of time

Thaya: human; mate to Aro

Thief: human; member of Olbar's tribe whose real name was taken from him; killed by Cutter

three-mating: a family arrangement where three elves choose to bond and live together

Timmain: elf; one of the High Ones; a self-shaper, she was the only High One who retained this power; became a wolf-in-form to help the High Ones survive

Timmorn (Yellow-Eyes): elf; A Wolfrider; the first chief of the Wolfriders; son of Timmain and a true wolf

Tolf (the Wood Cleaver): human; father of Adar

Toorah: elf; Sun Villager; mate to Suntoucher; mother of Leetah and Shenshen

toss-stone: a child's game in the Sun Village

treehorn: a large deerlike animal with antlers

tree-shaper: one who wields tree-shaping "magic," the ability to mold plant matter and to accelerate growth

Treestump: elf; Wolfrider; father to Dewshine; lifemate to Rillfisher; eldest of the current Wolfriders

tree-walker: one who is at home in the trees and who can move easily from branch to branch

treewee: a small, timid arboreal creature that resembles a perpetually miserable tarsier

Trial of Hand, Head and Heart: a Sun Village rite; a three-part contest by which two suitors for the same mate determine who shall woo the maid; the Trial of Hand is a test of balance, strength and dexterity; the Trial of Head is a test of wits and inventiveness; the Trial of Heart is a test of inner strength and peace

tribe-name: generally, the public name by which an elf is known ("Cutter" is a tribe name while "Tam" is a soul name); tribe names can be changed at any time

troll: one of at least two groups of beings (**holt trolls** and **northern trolls**) that have evolved from small, ape-like, burrowing creatures used by the coneheads as servants and mechanics on the palace-ship; it was a rebellion by the pre-trolls that caused the ship to crash on the World of Two Moons

Trollhammer: Dewshine's wolf

Tunnel of Globes: tunnel within Blue Mountain that leads to Winnowill's private chambers; it is lined with globes that explode when they are touched

Tunnel of Golden Light: tunnel that leads from King Greymung's throne chamber to the desert

Tunnel of the Green Wood: tunnel that leads from King Greymung's throne room to the site of the original holt

turn of the seasons: Wolfrider term for a year

Twen: Nightfall's soul name

Two-Edge: half elf, half troll; the hybrid son of Winnowill and an unnamed troll; his mixed blood, plus his mother's tampering, have had an unsettling effect on his mind so that he often seems insane; often speaks in maddening rhymes

Two-Spear: elf; Wolfrider; fourth chief of the Wolfriders; supplanted in that role by his sister Skyfire

Tyldak: elf; Glider; father to Windkin; because he wished to fly instead of simply glide, Tyldak allowed his flesh to be shaped by Winnowill into bat-like wings

U

Ulm: Redlance's soul name

V

Valley of Endless Sleep: name for the valley which contains the Forbidden Grove

Two-Edge

Winnowill

Vastdeep Water: Glider term for the great ocean that lies to the west of Blue Mountain

Vaya: elf; Go-Back; Kahvi's daughter; killed by Guttlekraw's guards

Voll: see **Lord Voll**

Vok: elf; Go-Back

W

wackroot: an herb with strong painkilking and restorative powers

Wadsack: northern troll; guard killed by Rayek and Cutter

Warfrost: Cutter's second and current wolf

Way, the: Wolfrider term for their general philosophy of life; the Way includes respect for nature and all life, and a certain adherence to tradition

whistling leaves: a medicinal plant with emetic and diuretic properties; its perforated leaves make a whistling sound when a breeze blows

Whitebrow: Clearbrook's wolf

whitecold: Wolfrider term for winter

whitestripe: a skunk

Windkin: elf; Wolfrider; son of Dewshine and Tyldak; a floater

Wing: elf; Wolfrider; son of Woodlock and Rainsong; currently lives in the Sun Village

Winnowill: elf; Glider; mother of Two-Edge; currently the lord — her choice of title — of Blue Mountain

wolf demons: human term for the Wolfriders

wolf-friend: Wolfrider term for their bond wolves

wolf nap: a short nap

Wolfpack, the: collectively, the wolves of the Wolfriders

Wolfriders: one of the tribes of elves living on the World of Two Moons; currently led by Cutter; more-or-less direct descendants of Timmain by her mating with a true wolf;

of all the elves in the world, only the Wolfriders are mortal by virtue of their mixed blood

wolf-send: a Wolfrider's method of communicating mentally to his or her wolf

wolfsong: a state of mind without past or future; the "now of wolf thought" or "always now"

Woodlock: elf; Wolfrider; lifemate to Rainsong; father to Newstar and Wing, plus an unnamed infant

World of Two Moons: the planet on which the Elfquest takes place

wormroot: a bitter plant eaten and enjoyed by the holt trolls

Woodshaver: Nightfall's wolf

wrapstuff: preserver term for the webbing that they spit to form their cocoons

Y

"yapthing": Petalwing's name for Choplicker
Yellow-Eyes: see Timmorn Yellow-Eyes
Yif: elf; Go-back; killed in the final battle of the quest

Yurek: elf; one of the Rootless Ones; Savah's lifemate; a rock-shaper, he created the Bridge of Destiny and died by leaping from it when it was finished

Z

zwoot: a large animal, part horse and part camel, used as a pack animal by the Sun Folk

zwoot (with rider)

Outroduction

March 16 — As I write I am sitting in a jet flying over what Native Americans humorously nicknamed The Valley of the Little Smokes. I've been in Los Angeles for a month now, visiting family and friends, doing business and finishing chapters six and seven of *Siege at Blue Mountain*. While I've been here, soaking up the sun and finding it a real challenge to keep on writing and drawing through a terminal case of spring fever, I met a lovely young woman named Kristi, a gardener whose skills and knowledge would impress Redlance!

To my delight I learned that Kristi had been reading *Elfquest* for years and was currently very interested in Father Tree Press's new book *Law and Chaos*. As we sat in the sun one morning, chatting over tea, she showed me a volume of computer generated photographs, vivid realizations of an intriguing and, for me, barely fathomable exploration called "chaos theory." The colors were electric, iridescent, oil on water, a pheasant's neck, the eye in a peacock's tail feather. And each photograph was the enlargement of a single detail in the previous one, the series going deeper and deeper, paisley and lace patterns stopping only when the color pages in the book ended and the text resumed.

Kristi opined that chaos theory, essentially the absolute necessity of randomness, applies to everything — gardens, ecologies of particular areas and their climates, human psychology, religion, the stars, and even *Elfquest*.

A good story is partly what it is and partly what its audience brings to it. Like those computer generated images, the simplest story has infinite layers, all randomly connected, though it may appear on the surface to have only one meaning.

Elfquest is ten years old this year, yet I am still amazed by the richness of interpretive insight that readers of all ages continue to bring to it. This is why I smile when colleagues ask me if I'm sick of the elves yet. Of *course* I plan to tell other stories featuring new and different characters — but — the soil of the World of Two Moons is still very rich, very fertile, and it has many gardeners. The loose ends I love to leave dangling in my plots are for clipping and replanting at a later time, by me or perhaps by someone else. Who knows?

1988 may turn out to be Richard's and my busiest year yet. While I, fink that I am, have been basking in California's spring weather, Richard has been holding the fort through one of New York's coldest, darkest winters ever, busily laying out the pages for the very *Gatherum* you hold in your hands. Apart from the improved and revised editions of the *Elfquest* color volumes, Warp Graphics and Father Tree Press will also publish a book tentatively titled *How to Draw the #!@*?! Elves*. Believe it or not, there is a formula for getting those maddening eyes and bodily proportions right. I'll be demonstrating that, along with lots of neat little technical drawing and cartooning hints not limited just to figures with pointed ears.

We're over New Mexico now and we've hit some turbulence. I love flying about as much as I love cleaning technical pens. Old, crusty technical pens.

But still, the cloud cover up here is something elves. From above, it looks firm enough to walk on. A High One could do it. Rayek, Skywise and even Winnowill all have the right idea, reaching for the stars. They all share the dream. But Kristi got me thinking — it just goes to show how different points of view can lend different colors and shades of color to the same dream. *Elfquest* is, after all, whatever it means to whoever reads it. And that makes it personal.

— Wendy Pini

144